M. A. WORRELL

Brutal Promise

First edition

ISBN: 979-8-9907498-0-1

This book was professionally typeset on Reedsy.
Find out more at reedsy.com

Contents

Chapter 1

Thank God tomorrow is the last day I'm going to find myself packed into this big city complex like a sardine in a can. The Farm Show is the biggest event of the year for us in sales, but that doesn't mean that I enjoy working at the stand every day as thousands of people crowd through. The orders for custom blade work are too plentiful to give up on coming here every year.

I miss the wild places where I can stretch out, let myself get lost, and breathe. Coming here is always taxing on my mind, and I can't wait to leave Harrisburg's sprawling city in the rearview mirror.

The large crowds that are drawn in every January fill me with anxiety as their loud chatter rings through the concrete rooms. I hope that tomorrow, being the last day, the crowds will die down some since I will be the only one working. Dad left around noon yesterday when Mom called saying the water pump on the well broke. Mom is plenty handy, but she is not mechanical which leaves her and the kids without water with another big snowstorm on its way.

What the hell was I thinking when I pitched the idea of being a vendor to this circus three years ago? Yeah, the number of sales has nearly doubled with our name being spread farther than our little town could ever hope to accomplish. Bringing me on as a full partner and expanding beyond Dad's simple fur trade has truly made a huge difference in our lives. Taking most of the financial burden from their shoulders makes me feel like less of a burden.

Finally, by nine the crowds have died, and I can close things for the night. Heading for my truck, I palm my keys as my eyes sweep the parking lot looking for any trouble. Thankfully, I don't hear anything out of the ordinary as I unlock the truck and climb inside.

My stomach reminds me that I haven't eaten all day as I shut the truck off in the hotel parking lot and the smell of food hits me square in the face. Like most cities, the hotel has a bar and restaurant next door.

I can't stomach the prices people pay at the complex for their food. I don't care if it's only once a year; it isn't that world-changing that I'll pay the outrageous prices they charge. No single patty with more bun than a burger is worth eight dollars.

I won't spend five dollars on a bottle of water either.

"Here's your whiskey, Ember," Mike says, setting the glass on a napkin in front of me.

"Thanks." I nod, not raising my eyes longer than needed before taking a sip of the drink and let it do its job. Every sip has the tension leaving my body bit by bit. I call for a second glass of whiskey as I'm finishing the last few bites of my steak. This next one should help me relax enough to sleep tonight.

"Good evening, beautiful," a silky voice interrupts my quiet as the barkeep comes over with the whiskey.

Presuming that the voice isn't talking to me but the leggy blonde three seats down, I pick up my drink. I'm here alone, and I am done talking to people for the day. Lifting my glass, I take a healthy dose as I relax back into my seat.

"It's a pleasure to see whiskey being so appreciated by such a lovely woman," the voice continues as a heavy hand settles on my shoulder before starting to slide down my arm.

Tensing, I jerk away from the unwanted touch. My face empties of any sign of emotion as my eyes narrow. "Not interested," I say before tossing back the rest of my drink in one go. The smooth burn helps settle my nerves.

The glass thumps against the bar, catching the attention of the barkeep as I pull out my wallet. Standing I put the chair between myself and Mr. Handsy.

Keeping him in my sight in the corner of my eye, I log his features into memory. It's the same man who tried to hit on me the other night when I came out of the bathroom. I didn't like his vibes then; I like him even less now. If a girl likes rail-thin blonde playboys with dimples, he would be their guy. Unfortunately for him, I want a man rough enough to throw me around like a rag doll.

The problem isn't that he's unattractive. He is remarkably good-looking on the surface; it's the inside of the man that has me putting space between us. For all his cool acts, I can tell he is a slimeball.

He chuckles, leaning against the bar and grinning at me. "Come on now, how bad would it be to sit and talk with me for a bit?" The grin he sports has my hackles rising. "What's your name, Honey?"

"I said I was not interested two nights ago. That is still my answer." I grind my teeth as I watch Mike print out the ticket with a frown. One lift of my finger and he'd be over to drop the prick on his head.

Another one of the many reasons I hate coming into the city is fools like this guy. Always thinking that they are God's gift to women. They make me want to puke or punch something. I'm sure I can make him look better if I reset his nose. Stupid entitled S.O.B.s. Every year I come down here they always try the same old shit.

Usually, Dad is quick to send them packing, but I'm on my own with him gone. That's not to say I can't easily deal with them. I just don't like to. In a family of military vets, no one grows up soft. Being female was no exception. I was taking my older cousins down before I was ten. Wish I was back home where one hard look sent all the idiots packing.

Finally, Mike brings the bill. Normally, I would wait for the change since money is tight at home, but I just want to get away from this guy before I'm forced to throw hands. "Keep the change, Mike."

My nod lets him know that I can handle the situation on my own. The man has known me for five years, so he gives me a small chin lift before getting called away to help someone else.

4

He's seen what I can do when needed.

His hand shoots out, latching onto my arm bringing me up short as I turn to walk away. "Now just a moment, Hun." He takes a step closer, a thin smile plastered to his narrow face. "I just want to talk. Won't bite unless you want me to." He grins wider, thinking his ass is funny as he rubs his thumb across the pulse on my wrist.

"Let go of me," I growl lowly. My head whips around with a snarl on my lips and fire in my eyes. Jerking my arm, I try to pull away from him. His touch feels slimy and invasive, causing bile to burn the back of my throat.

Surprised at my strength, I nearly knock him off balance, but he tightens his fingers, not letting me go. "Come on, Honey, what's the rush? I just want to talk. Come sit and have a drink with me."

He tries to pull me back to the chair, but I set my feet, refusing to move an inch closer. His fingers tighten, and I catch the brief flash of anger in his dirty brown eyes. "All I want to do is talk. No harm in that."

"It's only common sense to leave someone alone when they say no, or didn't your mama teach you that." This guy is pissing me off, and Mike is arguing with a man down the bar. "You'll be drinking through a straw the rest of your life if you don't leave me the hell alone!" I hiss balling up my fingers into a fist ready to knock his teeth down his throat.

Drawing my arm back to follow through with my promise, I'm stopped mid-draw. Large strong calloused fingers wrap over the top of mine as a large presence settles warmly against my back. Shock rushes through me, straightening my spine so a bare inch separates my body from the newcomers.

A hot breath whispers into my ear with a heavy Russian accent as the man's other hand settles in a light possessive hold on my left hip. "He is not worth the trouble of landing that hit, moy svirepyy kotenok."

Shivers race down my spine as my body naturally leans toward this new man's heat. A soft rush of air leaves my lips as my head tilts back to take in this new turn of events.

A glimpse of his face has me sucking in a sharp breath, filling my lungs with a wild spicy scent that has my body gravitating even closer to his. My back sinks into his hard chest as the heat from him somehow relaxes me, the tension in my body leaving me as my weight sinks further back against him.

He moves the hand from my hip around to my stomach to support the shift of my weight as my body melts into his. He brings our joined hands to the spot over my heart as he surrounds me with his body.

His lips skim my cheek as a silent groan vibrates through his chest. His nose dips, drinking me in. My breath stutters in my lungs as my mind goes blank to everything but him. Who the hell is this man?

"Forgive me for missing our dinner, sladkaya," he says crisply, allowing the other man to hear him. "My meeting ran later than expected."

Wrapped within this stranger's arms, leaning on his solid strength, all I can seem to do is stare up into the most chiseled, handsome face I have ever seen as I take him in. Dark hair, almost black, pulled back into a ponytail falls to his shoulders, making the heavy stubble that lines his jaw stand out.

Electrifying deep blue eyes that seem to burn brighter as soon as my wide hazel eyes lock with his. A shudder courses through my body as heat rushes through my veins straight to my core, hidden from the world by his encompassing embrace.

Breath infuses my starved lungs with fresh air only to freeze again as soon as he drops his face to bury his nose into my neck. The stubble of his jaw grazing sensitive areas makes me shiver as he lays a light kiss on my skin.

Taking a steadying breath, I shift. My body settles more firmly into his. If my left hand was free, I would lay it over top of the hand he is gently caressing my stomach with to stop the butterflies dancing in my guts. My body doesn't feel like it's my own. I've never responded to any man's touch the way I am right now.

"I told you already that everything was fine. Besides you're here now." I let a genuine smile pull my lips as I look up at him before brushing a light kiss along his jaw.

I could have dealt with the creep myself, but letting this Russian man in on the act could save me a hell of a headache. If I end up punching the creep, I'll have the pleasure of dealing with Harrisburg's famous police. A bonus is that this man is hot as sin, and my gut isn't telling me he's a danger to me. What's the harm in playing for a bit?

Chapter 2

Pulling my eyes from the gorgeous woman in my arms, I shift making sure that the gun handle at my waist doesn't press into her as she sinks further against me. I pin the man still holding her arm with a dark look. His eyes flash in understanding when he sees the look on my face. Good, he may be brighter than he looks.

H is mouth tightens, and his beady eyes flash as he struggles to keep a nasty look from his narrow babyish face. His stare bounces between both of us, looking for any weakness. His brown eyes burn with frustration as his jaw works back and forth wondering how to get what he wants. Men like him make me sick.

I let the threat of death leak into my eyes as I glare at him over the top of her head. "Is there a reason you still have your hand on my woman?"

My accent deepens as my anger builds when he continues to hesitate. My eyes narrow as I stare the fool down. "A woman should only have to tell you once. Yet here you are still touching what isn't yours without permission. I am not a man who shares."

He tosses her hand away as if it burns him and backs away, raising his hands as he does so. "Didn't know she was taken, man," he says though his eyes still linger on her soft body. Watching hoping for another chance to get close to her. Not in this lifetime, little boy.

A flash of burning rage rushes through my blood at his continued gaze on her while she is still in my arms. "As anyone can see she is a taken woman."

"There isn't any ring. I thought she was single." Small beads of sweat form on his brow and he shifts nervously.

Without taking my eyes off the fool in front of me I let go of her hand and fist the silky strands of her honeyed hair to tip her head back into my shoulder. Her arm moves so she can grab my jacket at the neck, pulling me closer. Her other hand slides down to splay over the hand on her gut pulling her body tighter against me.

"As you can see, she most assuredly is. We don't need rings

to know that we are taken. Do we, detka?"

She looks up at me, eyes shining as a breathless laugh bubbles out. "Who needs rings? Neither of us has looked at any other since we met. Besides you know what I would do to you if you ever strayed."

"You can bury those beautiful plans, moy sladkiy. You are all I will ever need."

Her hips tilt, driving back into my hardening cock, and a low moan slips from her lips. Smiling viciously, I run my nose up her slim neck, breathing in her woodsy scent of pine, wildflowers, and winter air as it pulls another primal groan from me.

How can this woman smell so good? Just her scent has me standing up, aching, and raring to go like lightning. My fingers tighten in her hair as my lips hover over hers, waiting for her to give consent before I take possession of them.

Electricity burns through my blood as her lips part in a deep moan. I deepen the kiss, and she opens her lips, allowing my tongue inside to taste the sweetness that is all her own with hints of whiskey. The taste is like nothing I've ever had before.

My arm curls farther around her middle, pulling her flush in my embrace taking note of the hard edges of the knife sheathed on her waist. She shivers in my arms before we both pull back. A pale blush stains her cheeks as my nose glides over the soft skin of her ear.

"Tak bozhestvenno." Leaning forward, my lips trail lightly across her brow. This woman could become addictive if I was a different man.

The fool's uncomfortable cough has me lifting my head to glare at him. His face burns red as his eyes dart between us. Heh, seems I made the little boy mad. He thought he'd get an easy piece tonight.

10

Chapter 2

Oh, how wrong he is. This is not the first time that he has tried to corner her, but it is the first time he hasn't taken the hint to back the hell off. In the few days I have been here, I have watched him walk out with a different woman every night.

All I was looking to do tonight was shower and sleep, but the sight of him touching her without consent had me seeing red. Her willingness to openly fight had me leaving the shadows before the thought of moving even had a chance to form in my brain. I'm lucky that he was too busy chasing tail to notice me or claiming to be her partner wouldn't be working so smoothly.

Chapter 3

Keeping a firm hold on the man's waist, I let him lead me out of the area. When he goes to put some distance between us, I don't let him, as the creep is still watching us through the windows. A sneer twists his face into a mask of fury, but he doesn't try to follow us.

Now that we are in the better lights of the lobby, I remember the man who still holds me to his side. The few nights I'd seen him, he'd been sitting in the shadows of the back wall, sipping vodka and working on his phone.

Seeing him in suits, I thought that he was a businessman;

the butt of his pistol seemed to point more towards a cop or private security. It would make sense with the influx of people during this time of year. Once he stepped in, Mick didn't throw another worried glance our way.

He allows me to take the lead with a lighter grip on my shoulder. Once in the elevator, I wait for the doors to close before addressing him. "You didn't have to step in. I'm not a damsel that is in need of saving."

His arm drops from me as I twist to lean against the wall. I hit the stop button to keep us closed in the private space and cross my arms, waiting for his answer.

"And let you deal with the police and bruised knuckles when I could easily redirect the situation? No, I don't think so."

"You think I can't handle the fallout?"

"No, sladkiy, it is better this way. I know that you could have had him on the ground very easily, but as much as watching you make someone bleed would make my night, you don't need the trouble." He grins, leaning back on the wall to mirror me.

"Wouldn't be the first time."

His head tips back laughing. Those big shoulders shake for a moment before he pushes off the wall, and he moves to stand over me with an arm bent above. "Are you in trouble with the law often, kotenok?"

"Only when needed." I like the fact that he has small nicknames for me even if I can't understand them. The low rumble of Russian that falls from his lips when he says those few words makes me want to smile each time.

Fingers brush over my skin as he pushes a hunk of hair out of my face. I left it down today in my rush to make it to my stand on time. Blue eyes lock onto the metal hanging from my ear. "Is the gun for these bullets hidden on your person like your knife?" He gives it a light tug with a smile.

"Wouldn't do me any good for these useless duds, now would it?"

"A woman who wears weapons of death so casually is not something I've ever run into in America. You make danger look like fun," he teases, leaning back to look me up and down slowly.

"Now that would entirely depend on my day and mood. You haven't traveled America as much as you think if I'm the first woman you've seen armed. Or maybe you have just been unobservant."

"Perhaps." He tilts his head acknowledging what I've said. "Maybe they just did not have anything to hold my interest."

"What makes me different from the thousands of women you've seen?"

"Your fight." His fingers wrap around my right hand. Bringing it up between us, he strokes the back of my knuckles. "Seeing the steel that runs under this delicate skin."

"Delicate?" Pulling my hand from his, I press both hands to his chest and step forward. He lets me push him back to the other side of the elevator until we are chest to chest. "I'm anything but easy to shatter."

His hands settle on my hips, holding me but not possessively. It's just enough for me to feel the heat of his touch. I like it. With each brush between our bodies, my blood comes alive. A feeling I haven't felt since the morning Jackson left my bed for the last time.

He must see the tiny flash of pain I don't catch in time because he straightens, leaning forward so that our eyes are level. "Where did you go, kotenok?"

"No where I want to return to." I steel myself again with a smile as I get lost in the color of his eyes. They remind me of a stormy sky.

"Someone hurt you; took your joy." The certainty in his words isn't untrue but just not the way he thinks.

"Long time ago." I wave my hand to show it doesn't matter any longer. "I'm content with what I have."

"Content is merely surviving, not living. What joy do you find for just yourself?" Fingers flex lifting the edge of my shirt while he waits for my answer.

Fuck, he goes right to the heart of something like a blood hound. Right now, I don't want to think. I want to shut my brain off and just feel. So, I do just that. Reaching up, I grip his jaw and pull him down to me.

He doesn't hesitate for a second as our bodies press close from tip to toe. Pulling away only far enough to speak he asks, "Are you sure that you want this?"

"Yes." Sealing our lips together, I moan at his taste.

Chapter 4

Mikhail

Triumph lights my blood as I hit the button for my floor. I don't stop kissing her, hands mapping her curves until the doors open. Breaking apart, I pull her down the hall to my door, unlocking it quickly before pulling her close again as I back her into the room.

I'm going to taste every inch of her sweet little body tonight. Without breaking the kiss unless necessary, we pull at each other's clothes until there is nothing left but skin. She isn't even startled by the sight of my gun as I set it on the dresser, but then again, she wears weapons every day, so the sight of mine is nothing new to her.

Palming her ass in my hands, I back her into the room further, covering her startled cry when her body tumbles onto the bed as I follow her down.

I work my way down her body, stopping to enjoy her lush breasts as I fill my hands with them. They don't stand as firm as other women I've been with, but they fit my hands perfectly. I spy small pale stretch marks as I roll her hard nipples between my fingers making her breath hitch as she arches up moaning for more.

Groaning, I pull one hard peak into my mouth, sucking roughly as she grips my hair with a startled cry pulling it fully loose to fall around my face. A sob sticks in her throat as I release one peak before paying the same attention to the other.

Her scream bounces off the walls as her body surges under the weight of mine. Her arms curl around my head pulling me down, demanding more as tears gather in the corner of her eyes. "Oh God!" She shudders in a shaky whimper.

Grinning, I leave her tits to make my way further south. My hands span her hips so I can shove her down into the bed as I nip my way over the matching marks lining her trim but plush middle.

My mother has the same marks spanning her body. Some asshole got her pregnant and left her. Irritation flares up as I knead the soft flesh beneath my fingers.

Tonight, I will fuck her so hard she'll be ruined for anyone after me. The thought of someone else seeing the beauty under me leaves a sour feeling in my gut. These feelings are not like me when I pleasure a woman, but I cannot stop them from forming, just as I cannot pull myself away from her responsive body.

Snarling possessively, I bury my nose in the nest of curls hiding the part I want the most. Pulling my right hand down, I spread her lips open for my view. She's soaking for me. The smell alone makes my mouth water as more moisture runs from her. Reaching forward, I lick her from bottom to top, making her buck and scream.

"You're so wet for me, baby girl," I groan, growing painfully hard from just the taste of her. My finger pushes into her wet heat, drawing another cry from her. It's so tight as she clenches around the single digit, I know I have to stretch her before I can fuck her, or I'm going to tear her apart.

Working another finger inside, I thrust them in and out as her grip grows so harsh on my hair, I'm sure she rips a fair amount from my head though I'm too occupied to care. Sealing my mouth over her clit, I suck in time with my fingers as I twist them before adding a third.

"Oh God!! I'm gonna...!" Her cry cuts off as she falls apart. Clamping down on my fingers as her cum gushes from her, flooding over my fingers. Her thighs locked around my head holding me in place as she trembles.

Pulling back after she calms a bit, I climb above her to take her mouth again. She clings to me as I take in her whimpers. I grab a breast and play with it as I start to work her up again.

"Please!" Her voice quacks as she shudders, pulling me closer as I feather kisses over her collarbone and up her throat.

"What is it you want, kotenok?" I tease, dragging my shaft over the gathering wetness. I nip at her neck, and she jerks as I suck the sting out of it.

"I need..." She drowns herself out in a loud moan as she rocks against my cock. "I need you ...in ....me. So bad," she whimpers.

"You need this, detka?" I ask, shoving two fingers back inside her.

"No! YES!! NO!!!" She yells bucking up into my hand even as she declares her denial. "You're driving me crazy. Please fuck me now!!"

Her nails dig into my back so hard I feel blood seep out as I pull my fingers away, quickly roll a condom on, flex my hips, line myself up against her, and shove my cock as deep as possible inside her strangling hold until our hips are grinding against each other.

Groaning, I have to still as I pant above her. The inner muscles of her cunt tighten harder as her scream fills the air. Her fingers clutch at me as she shifts under me. Gritting my teeth, I gently pull back and push forward once again.

"Bozhe detka…" I groan, leaning down to lap at her breast. "Ty takoy khudoy." I hold myself in control as we pant against each other, letting her get used to my size, but dear God, she feels like heaven.

Sweat runs down my back and shoulders, dripping onto her glistening body. Pressing over her, I lick the trails across her collarbone and down the valley of her perfect breasts.

"Please," she moans pulling her legs back and tilting her hips to grind against my pelvis. "Feels so good. So full…" Her body shakes trying to pull me deeper into her core.

Her eyes lock with mine, pleading as I hold myself back from pounding into her like an animal. Shifting, I reach up to palm the smooth swell of her neck as I spread out over her soft body.

"I've reached my limit, detka. You feel so fucking good and tight around me. I won't be able to be gentle as I fuck you," I growl in warning before I run my tongue to clean the sweat off the slim column of flesh in my hand as I tilt her head back.

Grinning, she grabs at my shoulders to lift herself off the

covers forcing me to brace myself to take her extra weight.

"I never asked for gentle," she purrs into my ear. "I want you to fuck me. Take me as hard and as fast as you can."

Her teeth close over my ear to scrape the sensitive flesh before biting roughly and my control snaps as I grip her neck harder and slam her head back into the bed with a feral snarl.

"Better hold on then, moy sladkiy." I grin before pulling back. I begin pounding into her scolding heat. My eyes nearly roll to the back of my head at the sweet hug of her flesh.

She keeps pace with each thrust until I grip her hips and lift them off the bed. She screams at the new depth, locking her legs around me as she begs for more.

Grinning, I let go of my last restraint as I pull her higher, hitting that secret spot inside her that makes her go wild. I feel her flutter around me as she gets closer with each savage plunge.

Suddenly her pussy clamps down on me like a vise and she arches into me struggling to hold on as the force of her orgasm twists her body beyond her control. She desperately pulls herself closer locking around me so I'm holding her full weight in my arms, forcing me to sit back on my knees.

Her teeth sink into my neck hard enough to draw blood but quieting the splitting volume of her scream as her body explodes within my hold.

The pain sends me spinning into my own orgasm, and I come with a roar, unable to stop. I buck up into her as I slam her down over my cock one last time and hold her there.

I've never lost myself so thoroughly in a woman in my life. I take her with me as I fall to the side before getting up to toss the condom in the trash.

Climbing back in the sheets beside her, I pull her limp body back against me and bury my nose in her hair. A soft sigh parts her lips as she fits herself closer. The tension from scoping out the latest target melts out of my body as sleep takes us still locked together. The fool will be dealt with tomorrow.

Chapter 5

My eyes slowly flutter open to the soft light of dawn. Sleepily, I shift, releasing several cracks through my bones before snuggling into the warmth against my backside. I can't believe how well I slept. My entire body feels soft and lazy, though my core is deliciously tender.

The figure shifts as two big arms curl around me pulling me back more firmly with a whisper of sheets. The unexpected touch startles me, and I try to jerk away only to be stopped by the immovable arms locked around me. The warmth mutters pulling me back, and a heavy leg settles over my own trapping me in place.

"Go back to sleep, detka," a deep gravelly voice grumbles into the back of my neck, bringing clarity to my foggy mind.

I remember the guy at the bar harassing me and then a sexy Russian man stepping in. His very presence calmed my battered soul and led to me letting myself go last night. A deep red flush heats my cheeks as I remember the pleasure he gave me.

It's no wonder I slept so deeply last night. I haven't been fucked so hard since Jackson came home from his first deployment. Smiling, I let my body relax back into his.

His arms squeeze me and his breath fans over my cheek as a contented sigh slips out when he nuzzles the sensitive skin behind my ear. At least until my eyes land on the clock and I see the time.

"Shit!" I gasp thrashing in his grip as I try to get up.

He mutters angrily as my head crashes back into his shoulder making us both wince. He pulls me to him and rolls on top of me, pinning my smaller body under his.

Small kisses brush lightly against my face and down my jaw. His teeth flash in the darkness of his stubble as he bites lightly at my neck. "It is early yet, moy sladkiy. Go back to sleep."

Trailing light kisses up my neck and along my jaw as he presses my body deeper into the sheets. "Unless you and this beautiful body are ready and willing to take more of me." His voice drops to a deep purr, making his accent even more panty-melting than it was last night.

A soft meow escapes me as my body arches up into his before I can pull myself together. Groaning, I push against him.

"Stop, please. I'm going to be late," I whimper as he bites my ear. Holy hell that feels good. "Please, I have to be at the complex in thirty minutes."

As much as I want to stay in this bed and even more so in his arms, I know that I must go because we need the final sales to keep us in the black for the next few months.

Groaning, he buries his face in my neck and takes a deep breath, pulling me closer. "Forget them and stay here." He breathes against my lips as his burning blue eyes meet mine.

Pushing him back I shake my head. "I can't." I turned my head to escape his kisses. "Please!"

I'm begging him at this point. I need to leave, or I'll throw myself at him. I can't believe how wanton I was last night even as the same urges rear their heads with each touch. I don't know the man, but my body couldn't fucking care less about that. It wants him now. Hell, I want him again, but I can't.

Snarling, he grabs a fist full of my messy locks forcing my head to still seconds before he lays a demanding kiss on my swollen lips. His tongue invades, pulling mine into a battle.

A moan rips from my guts as hunger hits me hard. My hands grip onto him as my senses completely leave me, and I push into him. I dig my fingers into his disheveled hair as I greedily drink him in deepening the hungry kiss.

He pulls away when I'm thoroughly breathless, unable to do anything but blink at him in a daze. His large hands brush the hair off my face before stilling to make sure my focus doesn't waver.

"Are you leaving tonight?" His breath rasps harshly in his lungs.

"No." I shake my head as I watch him.

"You will come back to this hotel," he demands, and I nod in agreement. He stares down at me as he considers something in his mind. After a moment he nods, giving me a long slow warm kiss. "I have meetings all day and will be back at nine. You will meet me in the bar for dinner when you get back."

Dumbfounded, I can only nod as he watches me. He takes another kiss before rolling off me to walk to the bathroom. My mouth dries out at the sight of his bare wide shoulders. Small tracks of blood on his back leading to the crescent shaped nail marks scattered over his shoulders and what looks like a bite on his neck. Did I really do that?

A ragged moan rattles my chest as my gaze follows the lines of muscles down his back to his gorgeous ass. I can't help staring at it as my mouth hangs open.

He spins around at my noise and instead of his ass I get an eyeful of his junk. Holy sweet merciful God in heaven that thing was in me last night. I'm fairly sure that I have drool running out of my hungry mouth as I forget about my time crunch to take all of him in. Is it wrong that I want to lick every single inch of him?

"Detka, you will not leave that bed today if you don't move your sweet little ass right now," he growls, eyes heating further, and a predatory grin stretches across his roughly stubbled face. He steps toward the bed, ready to fulfill his promise.

Lightning hits my system, and I vault out of bed, scrambling for my clothes. I pull them on, hurrying to look for my boots as he goes into the bathroom laughing. Finding them on opposite ends of the room, I pull them on and head for the door. As I grab the knob, ready to run for my room, he steps out of the other door and stops me with one look.

In two steps he's beside me taking hold of my arm in a firm grip as he pulls me close. His hand cups the back of my head as he lays a searing kiss on me. "Dinner." He speaks with a deadly serious tone. "Don't keep me waiting. I'm not ready to let you go yet." Hunger lights his eyes as my breath freezes in my lungs.

Still reeling from the kiss, all I can do is nod with a goofy smile before running out the door as he watches me go. I charge down the hall to my room which is surprisingly ten doors down from his. I hurry inside and rush to wash off and change my clothes for the day. Hurrying out the door, I head downstairs and grab some breakfast from the desk as I go.

After parking, I nearly sprint inside. There are already some people coming in and wandering around as I make my way through the halls, down the steps, and into the lower level where my stand is set up in the back.

Pulling the totes from under the table, I begin setting everything back up so the customers can see what I have left. I really hope I can sell out today. I'd love to go home with nothing but air and months of the books kept in the black for once. I can hear the volume of voices rise as the hour ticks on.

"Does the smith who makes these do custom work?" a man asks as he stops in front of me.

Smiling, I step forward. "Of course."

"Is he around to speak to, or do I need to reach out another day?"

"I can make anything you need within the laws of the state."

"Are you saying you made these?"

I have to hold in my amusement as his jaw literally drops open. Most people assume that I just work in the shop while Dad does the real work. In truth, it's the opposite. "Yes sir. From blade to sheath."

"You do beautiful work." He can't help but ghost his fingers over several of the knives.

"Thank you. Did you know what you were looking for?" I grab my sketch pad so I can make a rough sketch for him before he leaves.

Chapter 5

"I'd like an eight-inch Damascus skinning knife with a white oak handle. Is it possible to carve a deer scene on the handle?"

"What kind of scene are you looking for? Running, jumping, single, or a couple of deer? Do you have a deadline that you would need the blade done by?" After about ten minutes, we agree on everything he wants, when he wants it, and what it will cost to make the blade. So is my morning.

Chapter 6

M y contact gave me a book of information on the man that we were hired to track down and deal with. When the case was brought before us, I wanted to throw it out without looking into it any further. He seems far below anyone that we've ever personally worried about before.

Vlad, my oldest brother, is however our head pakhan, so these decisions are not for me to make. Now that I have him in my sights and watched the pathetic filth, I'm eager to pull him aside for a little chat. One that he will not easily forget.

Across the street, I watch him through the window of the rundown brick building he calls home. The heavy curtains would normally be enough to make me gag at the horrible 80's fabric if he wasn't pacing to the kitchen and back, screaming at the sad woman cooking. The bruise from yesterday is dark on her cheek.

He disappears from sight, and the door in the alleyway bangs against the blocks. Stomping out, he slams the door shut before slumping against the wall and lighting a smoke. His shoulders slouch farther as he takes hard drags. Tossing the butt on the ground, he shrugs a raggedy black leather jacket up as he starts down the street.

I let him get a few hundred feet down the road to make sure that he doesn't know that he's about to have the worse day of his life. Tracking him through this tiny city is so easy I worry that sleep will take me before taking him to my playground for the day to get better acquainted. The man hasn't changed a single part of his day in the time I've been watching him.

The ease of this target does not help keep my mind on the mission. Each quiet moment the sounds that she made last night fill the space. If I let my eyes close for even a second too long, I can picture her spread out, just waiting for me to take my time. Hell, I still feel the brush of her skin on the pads of my fingers. The juices dripping along her thighs.

Just before noon, I decide to make my move. This one is a creature of habit. He feels safe in his home territory, and that allows me to get close without him noticing. He approaches the back door of an underground club and pauses to light up another smoke. He pays no attention to the bodies that pass by him. The fool simply focuses on getting his lighter to work.

After several failed attempts to get the striker working on the cheap plastic, I walk up to casually offer him my own. I lean on the building next to him keeping my head bent. We don't need the pedestrians to get any hint of facial recollection should they look our way too closely.

He grunts leaning forward so the tip of the smoke catches the flame, taking a deep pull of fresh menthol into his lungs before leaning back to lunge back on the wall beside me.

"Thanks, man." He waves a lazy hand my way.

"No problem, Roch."

"Who the…" The surprise has him jumping forward. His head snaps back from the force of my fist before he can get the rest of the sentence out.

"No problem at all." I pat his back, letting his weight rest on me as a woman walking by glances our way. Wrapping my arm around his stunned form, I make my way back to my car. Opening the passenger door of the tan Buick, I dump his sagging body into the seat without a fuss and calmly get behind the wheel. A quick jab of the sedative from my pocket sends him into the dark for the drive ahead.

A short drive down the street and I pull into a parking garage transferring him into a black Dodge pickup. A few seconds to gag and tie him up, and then I drag him into the bed of the truck under the hard tunnel cover, slamming the tailgate closed before whistling my way to the driver's seat.

I follow the river south to drop out of the city before turning west. The bare trees lining the road are the only sentinels to the last ride of the scum in the back. The strong breeze the last whispers of freedom that he will ever have the chance to hear without any hint of fear.

Once I hit the dirt road, it's another few miles till I find the old steel building. It was a mill many years ago and now sits in ruins. It's been forgotten for decades since the coal plants were shut down.

The amount of rust on the door should be worrying. One scratch and you better hope that all your shots are up to date. Some might need it just by looking at the door. I on the other hand feel right at home in places like this.

Letting the tailgate drop, I reach in and grab the back of his leathers to drag him out. For such a skinny guy, he's got some weight to him as I heft him up onto my shoulder. He starts waking up as I open the rusty door to carry him into the dark room.

I let his kicking body fall heavily to the dirty floor. His body sends a big cloud of dust into the air around us, only to add more as he thrashes around trying in vain to gain control of his limbs. I stop myself from sneezing with a shake of my head to dissipate the air. Muffled screams of anger filter through the cloth holding his bug mouth shut.

Lifting a foot, I kick him hard enough that he flops onto his back, landing on his bound arms so they are trapped beneath him. He freezes as he sees me, staring up with fearful eyes for a few seconds before they harden, and I can see the threats, he wishes to volley at me.

"Before you say anything, Roch, or should I say, William Jemison. Which name do you prefer? I think I'll call you William; how about that?"

I tilt my head at him as I smile silently laughing at the garbled sounds coming from his gag. He struggles to get up only to stop as I place my shoe on his chest and press him back into the dust, leaning closer over him so that he can see how seriously my next statement needs to be taken.

"Your fate has already been decided. You will die in this

place no matter what you tell me." Reaching beneath my coat, I unsheathe my skinning blade. "How long and painful that death is going to be depends entirely on you."

A quick flick of my wrist opens a line of blood across his left pectoral that steadily seeps through his dirty gray shirt. He sobs as I rip the cloth from his mouth. "That was just so that both of us are on the same page. Now, who are you selling your supply to?"

"I don't know what you're talking about, you crazy asshole!"

"Tsk tsk." The blade flicks forward again, drawing a deeper line just below the original one and he screams like a toddler. "We know you sell drugs to a lot of groups, William. Groups that don't play nice with each other. So it's best just to come clean."

"Yeah, I sell, but I don't ask no questions. I get the money, they get the product. That's all I know!"

"Who do you supply?" My voice never rises above a casual conversation.

"I don't know. It's never the same guy or spot."

"Who do you sell to?"

"People, man. A lot of people."

"There's one group that likes to give it to the girls they take. Who are they?"

"I swear man, I don't know. Asking shit like that gets you killed, and I got a pregnant girl that depends on me!" His pupils are wild as they eye the knife in my hand. "Let me go, man. I'll give you all my stash. Just leave me and my girl alone."

"That girl doesn't seem to like you very much given' the beating you gave her last night for your supper not being warm. What kind of man strikes the mother of his child? Do you like hurting them? Possibly killing your child before it even has a chance to be born."

His face pales, his beady brown eyes growing too big for his face. My blade flashes five times to be echoed by a scream each louder than the last.

"Please stop!"

"Who do you supply?"

"I told you I don't know. Never the same person. Never the same number! I'm telling you I don't know anything about the group besides they buy a big batch every month." Snot and tears blur together on his face.

"When?"

"They just got a batch last week. They wanted it for this week. I don't know anything else, man. I swear that's all I know."

Frustrated by the truth I see in his face, I huff out a breath. Vlad is not going to be pleased. He wants names, and this fish isn't big enough to know anything useful. "Keep your mouth shut."

Turning away, I pull out my phone to call my brother. He answers right away. "Da."

"This one is too small."

"Move on and see what the next one has to tell us."

"Da. I will deal with it." The square of plastic returns to where it came from.

Guess my date tonight will be the last fun I will have for some time. I will have to make sure that we make the most of our last night together.

I return to the weasel with a large friendly smile. My knife flashes in the fading light. "Have the afterlife you deserve, William."

Chapter 7

Around lunch, Hannah in the booth next to mine refuses to let me go another day without eating while working, especially now that my dad is gone. She won't even let me pay for the meal that she brings me, so I grab the antler key chain she's been eyeing up all week with a wolf head carved into it and give it to her.

Before she lets me eat, she forces me to run to the restroom as she watches the stand for me. I make sure to get her number before she goes back to her alpaca yarn. I also make sure to buy three pairs of her winter socks as well since processed sheep's wool burns my skin.

I'm surprised when eight rolls around and the hall is nearly empty. There are only about twenty items that weren't sold at this point, so I decided to pack everything up. I'm proud of the number of sales and commissions that happened today. The commissions alone will keep us even for most of the year as long as I can get them all done on time.

Depending on the outcome of the trap line in the next two months we are going to be looking at a bumper year. The shop back home is in both dad and my name. The profits will be split between us and investing in some events further from home.

"Wow, you really sold a lot today, girl. I'm surprised so many people are out of tune with the wildlife around us." Hannah laughs looking at the small box that holds the furs, blades, and keyrings that didn't sell. "Which fur sells best for you?"

We grin at each other as I nod. "I know. I'm happy with how well we did. Last year wasn't as busy, so bringing so bringing more items with was a big gamble that has paid off."

We grab opposite ends of the table cover and begin folding it. "People are out of touch with everything that they can't have at their fingertips. Not something that makes me wonder too hard anymore. It is encouraging to see some younger ones take an interest in what I do. They sold me out of my coyotes yesterday.

"As long as I can get them all done on time, I think we will be able to finish out this year in black instead of red. It would be nice to have extra money this year to spend on the kids." I drop the cover over the items in the box and snap the lid closed.

"That's awesome!" She whoops giving a light jump which makes her blonde hair bounce as she comes to stand next to me. "I wish we lived closer to each other. I really enjoyed getting to know you this week."

"We'll have to work something out. It's going to be hard to get a hold of me for the next couple of months with me out on the line. As soon as I get back in, I'll call you up."

Finding people outside of my small town who I enjoy being around is difficult for me. But after some talking, we discovered that we are both from small mountain towns that found each of us just a little strange.

Hannah lives like a hippie in an extremely conservative area and is always running around at top speed. I love my town and have always been close to its residents. At least until I returned home after Jackson's death. I wasn't the carefree girl that they all knew. I became quiet and withdrawn. I disappeared into the mountains and made them my home. Where most try their best to avoid, I thrive in the hostile areas. They make me feel alive. More like my old self.

Hannah, though, is like a ball of sunshine while I like to sit in the shadows and watch. We were friends within the first hour. I really am going to miss her. We say goodbye, making sure that we have the correct numbers to keep in touch before going our separate ways.

Stacking all the boxes inside each other, I carry them out to the truck in one easy trip. Feeling good, I climb into the old rust bucket and make my way back to the hotel.

I park the truck and sit in the parking lot for a moment. Leaning further back in my seat, I bite my lip as I remember the demand for dinner tonight. That's what it was a clear demand. No 'will you' or 'if you are able'. It was 'you will be there to eat with me at the assigned time'.

Can I really face him again? Should I simply grab my bag and hit the road this minute? The memory of last night will always be burned into my brain. I felt like a different person the whole time. Six years without wanting a man's touch, and after one night, I want more with this man.

There was something there. Something that seems to settle in place when we touch. Like we'd known each other forever. I know I'm a broken mess on the inside. Jack's death shattered my world, and I'm not sure that I am fully healed.

Plus, I have kids. What man wants to take care of someone else's children? Even if I did want more than tonight, it wouldn't be fair to expect more from him.

We don't even know each other's names, but when he asked me what joy I took for myself, my mind went blank. No one has ever asked me that. I had planned to tell him about my kids but stopped myself. This man will be out of my life after tonight. He doesn't need to know about them.

I love my kids, but all the smiles and laughs were shared with the rest of the family. I always wish Jack was here to see this. Jack would be so proud if they did this or said that. But mostly, I am sorry that my wonderful man can never make these memories with our kids. I can't remember ever taking some spare time or buying some silly thing that caught my eye.

Who is Ember Lee Russell anymore but the lonely eccentric widow who disappears into the woods for weeks on end while her parents watch her children? It caused even more gossip when I took the kids into the forest with me. I had lost myself in my grief. I still work, am a mother, and I do it all with a smile. Starting this moment, things were going to change. I will always move heaven and earth for them, but I was going to discover myself again.

Determination fills me as I head inside. I stop at the entrance of the bar, looking around for my date. When I don't see him, I'm not too upset because I know that I'm early by nearly twenty minutes.

Stepping back, I head into the hotel. I decide to go up to my room and get cleaned up before meeting him. The elevator opens when I'm halfway to it, and out steps the creep from last night. That's just what I want to intrude on my good day. I see him grin as he catches sight of me just as I spin to make my way to the restroom. Only a few more steps and I can hide in here until he leaves.

Just before I step in the doorway, a force pulls my gaze up to the front doors to see my Russian mystery man walking through. Relief flushes through my veins as I alter my course to collide with him.

A teasing smile tips my lips, I call out a few feet from him. "Hey, honey! I'm so glad you didn't have to work late tonight again, handsome."

His dark head snaps in my direction with a tiny predator's smile, but he must see the irritation I try to hide. His eyes flick to look behind me and harden for a moment before he looks at me again with another hungry smirk.

Lengthening his stride to meet me he lifts his arm, allowing me to curl into his side under his wide shoulder as he pulls me possessively to him. My arms curl haphazardly around his wide shoulders to grip the back of his head holding him close. He dips down to claim my lips in a deep brutal kiss that has me melting into him further. Yep, there's no way I'm not getting another night with him.

Nipping my bottom lip, he moves his mouth to my ear as he whispers, "Never late when I have you to look forward to, detka." His other hand cups my cheek as he lays several small kisses just behind my ear all while holding me in place.

"Sweet talker." Sliding up I lay a kiss on his jaw.

A chuckle rumbles through his chest when I wiggle within his hold before his voice darkens and he pulls me closer, his lips ghosting over my ear. "Did he touch you?" With each word, his voice sounds darker, deadlier, sexier. Good lord, I think I'm deranged as my blood tingles in my veins with heated pleasure.

"No," I sigh, looking up at him as his scent settles into my lungs. What the hell kind of body wash does this man use, or is it just him? I don't know but I want to bottle it up and soak in it. Did I just lick my lips again?

Humming, he leads us past the creep standing by the desk acting as if he doesn't notice us. My arm curls under the back of his buttoned-up suit jacket, letting my fingers graze the top of his belt. I feel the bulk of his pistol and smile even more. Dangerous men do not scare me. They never know that I'm just as deadly if not more so than they themselves are.

Small mountain towns are home to the toughest people around. Most of the people have lived there for generations. When the mines dried up, those who didn't have the grit and determination to live off the land left. It made us hard and rough. All my family has a military background, and though I never served, they taught me what they learned. I'm not afraid to take on someone bigger than me.

Feeling bold, I wedge my fingertips into the space between his body and pants just beside his weapon. The heat coming from him is so intense it chases away the residual unease of nearly running into that asshole again. I smile up at him as he glances down at me in question before chuckling.

The heavy arm that hasn't left my waist the entire time lifts to stroke gently through my hair. Cupping the side of my head, he leans down without breaking stride to kiss my head lightly before his breath whispers down the side of my face. "We were too busy last night to get names, moy sladkiy. Tell me." Again, it's a demand, not a question.

Laughing, I shake my head at his cocky attitude, teasingly bumping my hip into his which he lets me move just the slightest bit. He tightens his grip on my hip. "Ember."

His blue-gray eyes light up brighter as he smiles down at me. "Hmm, Ember." His accent gives my name a husky twist that wakes up certain parts of my body I didn't know existed until last night. Now it seems they don't know how to turn off.

"Fitting for my little fighter. Moye malen'koye plamya fits you much better." His other hand reaches up to catch my chin as he brings us to a stop. Turning so our fronts are pressing together, he lowers his head just shy of another kiss.

"What does that mean?"

"My little flame."

"Hmm...I like that. And you?"

"Mikhail," he says, gripping tighter. "You'll be screaming it before the night is over. First, I must feed you as promised. You'll need the extra energy." His dark promise is sealed with another kiss before he turns to take us into the bar.

Snickering I cover my mouth as he pulls out a chair and settles me at the table before seating himself. I swear this man is so full of himself but at least he can back up that talk in the bedroom.

"Will I now?" I smile, tilting my head to watch him.

Chapter 8

"What can I get you started with today?" Her bubbly voice grates on my nerves for some reason as she quickly skips over me to flutter her lashes at Mikhail. Her lips pout, hoping to draw his attention away from me. I find myself narrowing my eyes at her. She simply ignores me yet again.

Ignoring her failed attempts to engage him, he smiles at me. "Whiskey again, moye plamya?" he asks, accent deepening to a heavy purr as he laces our fingers in a clear message to the girl, which she obviously ignores.

His eyes never leave mine as I nod. "Good, and I will have your best vodka." He tips his head in a nod at the girl as she smiles before leaving. "So, tell me, Ember, how was your day? Did you sell everything as you hoped?"

"No, not everything. I have half a tote left to take home with me, but it's more than I ever thought I'd sell here. We've had a good start to the year so far." I smile at Mikhail, happy that he would have the thought to ask me how my day went. Also, that he picked up without asking that I was working and not out buying useless things.

"And how many totes did you bring with you this year?" Mikhail asks squeezing my fingers tighter as he shifts forward in his chair giving me his full attention. His blue eyes glitter in good humor as the waitress brings our drinks and sets them in front of us.

"Are you ready to order?" she asks, smiling shyly at him without looking at me yet again. Jealousy flares as she eyes up my man. Whoa, where did that come from? I have no claim on his gorgeous man.

"What would you like, sladkaya," he asks without looking at the waitress yet again.

Smiling, I look at him, laughter in my eyes because I know he sees how jealous I am. He's just going to let me sit here knowing that he's not interested in what she has to offer.

Put at ease, I tell her without any heat between us. It's what I had last night, but I don't like the other fancy things on the menu. Well, except for the cheesecake, and who can refuse a good cheesecake? It's not like I get it very often back home. I've held myself back by not ordering any all week, but tonight I'm going to indulge a little.

Smiling he still doesn't look at the waitress as he speaks. "I'll have the same."

"Of course, sir." She nods as she looks sadly at him. She really is pretty with blonde hair in a pixie cut. Light freckles dust her cheeks, and her eyes are a light sky blue. Mikhail doesn't look anywhere but at me the entire time. I'm not sure why he favors me over her, but it's nice to have a man's full attention. I haven't even entertained the thought of men since Jackson was killed. Most of the time they just irritate me.

"So, what do you do?"

His rich chuckles send shivers down my spine. "I oversee several construction companies that my father started many years ago when he moved to New York. He and mother have since returned to Moscow."

"What kind of construction?"

"It depends on the bids that come in. We do most anything."

"I'll have to keep that in mind. I know of plenty of people who I could gift your services to."

"Why do I get the feeling that they would not like your kindness." His eyes glitter in amusement while he leans back to study me.

I laugh without answering. There are plenty of people who I would truly help, and some that I would help to make my day more entertaining. Small towns have their fair share of nosey old biddies, and I am a large center of their rumor mill.

"Tell me, moye malen'koye plamya, what is it that you do to keep yourself busy?"

"My father and I own and work a trapline. Along with working the pelts of our catches, I forge knives. That's actually the reason that I'm in this damn city even though it makes my skin crawl every time. It was quite profitable this year. If I remember the count correctly, I have fifty custom blades to make when I get home."

"And this is a good business? I did not know that Americans still did such trades." His brows rise in disbelief even as he nods along with me.

"It's not as widely known anymore, I'll give you that, but there are more people than anyone realizes that refuse to buy from the big brand names in the knife world. The fur industry is still very small, but I can see it slowly coming back."

"Hmm, I would like to see that. Nothing is as warm as a good fur coat. Too many young people yelling about the inhumanity of real fur, but at least it isn't sitting in a landfill for the next two hundred years like the fake trash they are so proud of."

"I agree. That fake shit is nasty. I can work a line in negative 10 without being cold in my grandfather's furs."

We talk through the next hour about anything that comes to mind. He's so easy to talk to that I think very little of watching what subjects are brought up between us. I don't tell him about the kids because he doesn't need to know about them. All that's left between us is the night ahead, and then we will go our separate ways. We both have a better understanding of each other. It's comfortable just the two of us.

Pushing my plate away, I pick up my fifth whiskey and drain the last bit in the glass before I settle back to watch him. It doesn't take him long to notice and look up at me. Pushing his own now empty plate away, he reaches for his fourth glass of vodka, but I cut him off.

Reaching forward I knock his hand away and grab the glass myself. A look of wondering fills his face as he cocks a brow before leaning back to watch me. I grin at the challenge with a wink. I tip the glass in a salute before tossing the alcohol back and letting it burn down my throat as I lick the taste off my lips.

Chapter 8

His eyes blaze and his nostrils flare as he shoves his chair back even as he pulls money out to throw on the table. Pulling me out of my seat so fast I would stumble if he let me go.

Instead, he pulls me closer as he heads for the door. His hold is firm but not painful as he leads me along. Giggling I lengthen my stride so I can press against him even though I don't feel the cold January air. We don't waste time finding the elevator.

I feel bold and free. My fingers drift down his chest, and lower to feel the strength hidden under his clothes. I grin at the shiver that runs through him. It's going to my head to have this sort of power over a man I've just met. I may also be slightly drunk for the first time in years.

As soon as the doors close us into the small car, he spins me around. My back presses into the wall as his hand takes hold of my throat. Boldly unafraid, I stare unblinkingly into his eyes as my hands drift lazily up his arms to settle around his broad shoulders.

Letting my fingers flutter around the hair at the base of his neck, I relax into his hold to tilt my head back with a smile. "Kiss me," I demand, lifting my lips for him.

A feral grin lights his mouth as his fingers tighten around my neck before he covers my lips in a bruising kiss that instantly leaves me breathless. Dear lord, this man can kiss.

Moaning, my mouth opens inviting him in without any hesitation. Heat flares in my core, and I want even more. I need more. Lifting my leg, I hook it around his thigh, so his leg is positioned to rub against where I need him.

He grips my leg, lifting it higher as he shoves his own forward. My shoulders are pulled down as he does this giving my hips the perfect angle to grind against him.

He breaks the kiss with a deep purr. "Fuck! Rub the sweet

pussy against me just like that. Such a good girl for me, moye malen'koye plamya." His mouth travels south to my neck as he rocks the full length of his hard cock against my hip.

I'm so turned on and wet from him and his dirty words it's amazing that I'm not soaking the whole of his leg. A yelp echoes in the space as he grips my ass with both hands lifting me higher so I can wrap my legs around him.

The new angle has us both moaning as he shifts, moving his dick directly against my pussy. We start grinding together through our clothes. A harsh rumble vibrates his chest as he grips me harder.

I'm sure I'll be bruised as hell tomorrow, but fuck if I care. If I wasn't so hot and bothered right now, I could kiss him all day and never find it any less addicting than the first time. However, I do want more, and I will be damned if I don't get it soon.

The ding of the door has him pulling his mouth away as the couple on the other side let out scandalized gasps as they stare at us. Grinning without one ounce or shred of embarrassment, he does not put me down but carries me out the door and down the hall.

Leaning me against the wall, he fights the lock with numerous curse words while I scrape my teeth over his pulse before biting into the flesh. As soon as it clicks open, he takes us through and uses my back to slam the wood shut.

I'm leaning against the door, trapped and held up by my grip around his shoulders and his hips pressing into mine as his hands rip open my shirt. He makes quick work of the button and zipper of my jeans before he tugs them off my ass.

Gasping, I fight to grip him tighter as he pulls my legs closer together to pull the material mid-thigh, leaving me with less of a grip but too wired to care about anything but him inside of me. I trust him not to let me fall.

The click of his belt buckle is the only warning I have before his hips thrust wildly, sinking his entire length in me. The brutal force of it has my head slamming off the door and a scream flying from my lips. Damn, the burn of stretching feels so good.

Hips strain against the restraint of my pants, wanting to be closer to him. Greedy lips attack every inch of skin they can reach as his whiskers leave burns across my chest. My fingers grip his hair as my elbows lock behind his shoulders to pull him deeper into my breasts. Obligingly, he immediately sucks one hard peak into his mouth with a growl. The suction alone could probably kill me right now.

"Let me hear you!" he snarls, gripping me harder. His hips speed up, setting a brutal pace I have no hope of matching with my legs cuffed in my jeans. "Let this whole fucking city hear how much you love my cock pounding this tight little pussy."

Never thought I was one for dirty talking in the bedroom, but his words ignited a fire within me. The demand washes through my blood leaving me wetter than before as I gush around his girth. The sounds I unknowingly held back break free as my body trembles against his. A scream of pure ecstasy accompanies each delicious drag of his length as he powers into me.

"OHHH... Fuck Mikhail! So close." Tossing my head forward onto his shoulder, my breath hitches and stutters as I get closer.

"Scream for me," he growls pressing me harder into the wood. "Cum for me, moye malen'koye plamya." His teeth lock onto my neck making explosions ignite, and I scream louder than I ever have. My nails bite into his shoulders as I fall apart in his arms. The world turns white, and all sense of being is lost.

After a few moments, my body calms, and I blink. I'm still

tightly wrapped within his arms with him leaning against me blowing like a freight train. With a deep breath, he shifts to lift me off the door. Heading for the bed and spreads me out on top of the duvet before pulling his slightly softening cock free of me.

Groaning, I reach for him not ready for things to end. "Mikhail…"

With a deep rumble of amusement, he grabs my wrists in one big hand and lays them above me on the bed. "Don't move them from this spot." He squeezes them for emphasis before letting go to trail his fingers from the tip of my fingers and down the entire length of my body.

With ease, he slips my tangled jeans and panties off. Lifting first one leg and then the other to his shoulders he rubs at the red marks left by the heavy denim. His eyes lift to lock with mine as he leans forward, settling himself between my open thighs. Licking his lips, he grips my hips, raising me up with seemingly no effort.

A deep breath pulls through him just before he drags his tongue along my dripping seam. "So sweet." He groans, closing his eyes in bliss as he continues to lap at me.

Yelping in surprise, my hands fly over my head in search of him needing to ground myself as electricity fires through my veins. Before they can catch him, a sharp slap stings my lower lips making me scream as my hips buck up at the new sensation.

"Hands back where they belong. We are just getting started."

"Fuck…" I pant forcing my arms back to the bed. "Please!"

The vibration of his amused chuckle sets off new fireworks in my core as he pushes his face back into my pussy. "Don't worry we have all night to get to that part of our fun, Ember. There are hours left for me to explore this delicious body."

Chapter 8

"Are you trying to kill me?" My laugh is mostly airless because I can't seem to catch any air from my burning lungs.

"Never, moye plamya. Now lay back and let me feast."

Chapter 9

Stretching I roll over wrapping myself around the hard warmth of Mikhail's body. Muscles pulse reminding me of every delicious dirty thing he put me through in the hours since we crashed into the room.

I should be sleeping soundly after being taken so many times without mercy, but my body is still vibrating. I know I can't take more if I want to be able to walk tomorrow, but he hasn't let me explore him as much as I wanted during our fleeting time together. I want to taste him so much it hurts, and well, he's still passed out beside me. No time like the present to get my fix.

Lifting a hand, I trail my fingertips lightly over his shoulder and begin tracing them over the dark lines that I can make out in the dark of the room. It's not enough to identify what the ink designs are but at this point, that isn't what I want. He shifts with a small mumble before rolling to his back still holding onto my hip.

Smiling, I push closer as I lift up on my elbow to press a kiss over the long rigid scar just above his heart. My hands drift over him admiring his strong toned body. He doesn't have the sculpted body of someone who works out, but each and every muscle looks like it was earned through hard demanding work.

Meanwhile, my desire to taste him has me licking over another tattoo that spans from his shoulder down the whole right side of his chest. Just like my favorite ice cream, one taste isn't enough. I continue using my tongue to map him until I find his small nipple. Flicking over it for a few moments before taking it into my mouth to suck on it. His chest tightens causing my teeth to scrape it lightly.

He jerks awake under me. "Ember," a harsh whisper husky with sleep makes his accent very heavy. It's incredibly sexy. "What are you doing?"

"Snacking," I whisper as I slowly creep down his body. "I woke up hungry." Letting my lips trail down his side to keep contact with him.

"Hmm. Did you now, malen'koye plamya?" Husky chuckles drift around us. His hand settles on the top of my head fingers threading into my hair following me as I slide my way down to his hips. "I'm sure I feed you quite well."

"Mm hmm…You did, but I woke up hungry. Do you want me to stop?" I nip along the muscles of his defined abs before continuing. My fingers wrap around him as I take my first good lick along his length. I never understood why women seemed to like this so much, but now all I want is to continue tasting his sweet salty tang.

His thighs flex, falling open with a groan allowing me to settle more fully between them. Taking the head of him into my mouth as he grunts.

"Fuck no." His big fingers push on my head in encouragement, though I don't need any. "Don't stop, or I'll beat your sweet little ass red. Your mouth feels so fucking good around my cock."

Instead of answering, I snicker at the needy demand before taking him deeper into my mouth. Lifting my arms, I let them trail down his chest. Hooking my fingers to scratch along his sides, making his big body shiver under me. For once he lets me take control. I'm bound and determined to make the most of the opportunity. I tease him. Alternating between sucking and licking.

His breathing is quickly turning harsh. Fingers clench and unclench in my hair following my movements. His hips jerk up into me unable to stay still as he moans. "Fuck Ember. You are doing so good."

A heavy groan fills the room as he grips my head holding it still as his hips drive faster, hammering into me as if I'm not on him at all. Grabbing the base of the shaft in my mouth is the only thing that keeps me from choking on him.

"Yes, detka! Take all of me. Swallow every last drop!"

He growls as he loses control. Every stroke bounces off the back of my throat. I struggle not to gag on his length. Soon my mouth is flooding with his cum. I swallow as quickly as I can, taking every drop he gives me. After a moment, his rigid body goes limp as he sags back into the mattress.

His hands blindly grab hold of me. Gripping my sides, he pulls me into his arms wrapping me up against his pounding heart. His hands grip my hip and shoulder to hold me flush against him. Taking possession of my mouth he kisses away the last of his cum. Sighing, I relax into him.

"I trust your desert was filling." His breath ghosts over my neck before his lips brush over my pulse.

"Perfect as the cheesecake," I say smugly, wrapping myself around him.

Husky chuckles fill the air around us as he hugs me. "Such a good girl for me." Turning so we're on our sides, my back to his front, he curls around me, laying a gentle kiss on my hair before relaxing.

For now, I'm at peace with everything in my life. It's not hard when the man holding me captures my attention and refuses to let me be anywhere but completely with him in every way. Maybe one day, I will find a man who brings out this side of me again, but I don't think it will ever happen. God breaks the molds after making men like the ones I've been lucky enough to have in my life, no matter for how short a time.

Forcing my mind to release all the flying thoughts in my head, I curl further against Mikhail and tell myself to relax. Both of us sink into sleep once again.

Soft rays of sunlight greet me when I open my eyes again. Mikhail is sleeping soundly, wrapped around me in the dark room. Closing my eyes, I sink into his embrace, content to simply lay here in his arms for just a little longer.

Chapter 9

After what seems like only a few minutes, my eyes open again. I look at the clock on the nightstand to see sunlight filtering through the room. It doesn't shock me as much as it fills me with disappointment when I see that it will soon be time for me to hit the road.

For the first time in years, I feel safe and at peace with myself. I wish we could have a bit longer together. Tears mist my eyes, but I refuse to let them fall. Easing myself from his embrace, I get up and start gathering my clothes.

I have to stop and look back at the sleeping form one more time. I hungrily drink in the image of him laid out on the bed, the white sheet laying dangerously low over his hips as he rolls to his back with a grumble throwing an arm over his head. I study each inch of him to commit him to memory.

He lived up to his promise. He made me forget everything but him during our time together. Only I think he has ruined me for any other man but him. Which is fine; I do not need another man in my life. Jackson and Mikhail have already given me enough good memories to last a lifetime. Smiling, I brush the burst of sadness away as I turn and close the door on our chapter together.

Grabbing my things from my room, after a quick shower, I headed for the front desk to turn in my key. Digging into my bag, I come up short when my fingers brush over the soft fringe. Frowning I lift the item out, wondering why one of my dream blades is in my bag. Shaking my head, I push it back in and finally find my keycard to check out.

Turning away from the desk, I reach into the bag for my keys, but I'm brought up short when my fingers wrap around the sheathed blade again. My fingers lightly trace over the etching and stitches as I close my eyes. Mikhail's face grins back at me with each pass over the blade.

Pulling in a deep breath, I grip the blade and head out for my truck. Unlocking the cap hatch, I open the tote that holds the extra padded boxes. Grabbing one, I settled the blade in the lining and turned back to the hotel.

"Hello mam, did you forget something?" the clerk asks with a smile.

"Yes, I was eating dinner with the gentleman in 408 last night, and I found something of his in my bag. Did he happen to check out yet?' I am proud of myself for speaking so clearly.

"No, he hasn't come down yet," she says after looking at the computer. "Would you like me to give it to him for you?"

Pulling my lips into my teeth, I think it over. I want to make sure that it does end up in his hands. Could I see him again without wanting more time with him though? Could I hand him this and simply walk away? "Thank you. That would be wonderful." I smile as I hand the box to her.

She takes it from me and attaches a note with his name and room number. "Of course. No problem at all."

Miles out of the city and across the Susquehanna, I pull into Liberty Station and park in the back of the lot. The tears I wouldn't let fall now stream down my face, and nothing I do can stop them. It doesn't matter that I don't really know the man. Mikhail has taken a large piece of me with him, but he's also given me some of myself back.

I have become so tied to the past that I have neglected to live in the now. Whenever I felt like the world was closing in on me, I took off for the lines. Sometimes going so far as to live off of what little I carried on my person.

Chapter 9

"Pull yourself together, Ember," I grit out as I grip the steering wheel. "It couldn't have ended any differently." Neither of us promised anything more than what is already behind us. It doesn't make the hurt lessen any as I tell myself to move on.

Wiping the breakdown from my face, I take a breath and set the truck into motion again. Stopping, I wait for it to clear enough for me to pull out. For a moment I stare south, wishing some things in my life were different. "Goodbye, Mikhail, and thank you."

My breath leaves me in a broken exhale. It's time to get back to my life. I don't have the time or luxury to sit around missing a man. Pulling myself together, I check the road before heading north again. Memories of our night flash in my mind. Frustrated, I turned on the radio and let Merle and Cash carry me on my way.

Chapter 10

Ember's soft tear filled whisper jolts me from a dead sleep to protector mode in least than a heartbeat. Instinctively I reach to pull her under me as my other hand brings my pistol around, safety off. Without her filling my arm I roll to my feet senses scanning the room for what woke me and coming up with no threats.

"Ember," I say searching the small room before going for the door to check the hall. "Malen'koye plamya." The hallway is as empty as my room no matter how much I wish it to be different. Cursing, I slam the door closed.

Everything of hers is gone. Bitterness fills me as I pull on the clothes from last night. Where the hell is my shirt? A glance at my phone shows it's after eleven. I should be on my way back to New York already since I finished our business yesterday. Damn, I'm not looking forward to speaking with my brother.

One taste of Ember's sweet body had not been enough. Even now, I still crave the taste and feel of her. I can't remember a time when I took a single woman so many times. I got what I wanted and left. There were never any repeats with any woman over the years.

Aggravated by my own actions, I drop onto the bed and tie my shoes. It's for the best, I know. Bringing a woman into my world who isn't already a part of it hardly ever ends well. My world is hard, and only the strongest survive. Standing, I set the room straight still looking for my shirt. I don't see it anywhere.

Lifting the blanket, a shirt falls out of the tangled mess. Picking it up, I frown before starting to laugh because it's not mine. This is Ember's. Setting it aside, I finish picking everything up, but my shirt is still missing. Picking up her shirt I bring it to my nose and inhale her heady wild scent.

There's no way she left this room without a shirt, which means she has mine. Amusement seeps through me. Whether by accident or design, the little minx left with more than just memories of me. A twisted sense of pride grips me, knowing that she has something of mine. Chuckling I pull my spare shirt from my bag.

What's the loss of a two-hundred-dollar shirt to me anyway? Yesterday's job had made a mess, and I had changed well before returning to the hotel so there is nothing on that shirt but me. Picking up my bag and her shirt, I bring it to my nose again before stuffing it into my things. Turnabout is only fair.

Closing the door, I head for the front desk. Pulling the key from my pocket, I slid it across the desk with a nod to the receptionist. Turning I make for the parking lot ready to head home and update my brothers about what I found out from the little mole the Armenians tried to plant in our operations.

"Excuse me, Mr. Sokolov sir." The receptionist hurries after me, so I stop to wait for her. "Excuse me, sir. The lady you were with last night said that this was yours."

I look down at the box she's holding out, knowing that it isn't anything of mine. What did Ember leave for me? Taking the box from her hand, I give her a nod before heading for my car. Climbing behind the wheel, I toss the bag in the back before I sit there, staring down at the box.

A small seed of doubt flickers to life. Maybe she was a decoy to get my attention. The way she responded to me the last two nights leaves my gut telling me she was being true. However, in my world, you can't be too careful. The thought of hunting her down leaves a rotten feeling in my gut. Please don't let me be wrong about this woman.

Gripping the string, I pull it off and open the lid. A piece of padded velvet lays on top. Carefully I lift the fabric to look underneath, and my breath catches. Nestled in the folds on the bottom is a sheathed knife. The sheath is hand-tooled and polished in a light butternut color. The handle is an antler with a scene carved in it.

Picking it up, I take a closer look. One wolf stands over two small pups as another stands in front of them against another wolf. The wolf guarding the one with the pups has a small blue gem as an eye as it stands against another wolf with a yellow eye. I pull it free of the sheath in awe of the handles fit in my hand before I test the balance of the blade. It's nothing less than perfect, and the blade is razor-sharp.

I'd been amused at her claim to be a trapper and blade smith last night. Laughed at her, really. I thought she worked in a shop and did not actually make the blades herself.

Now with the proof gleaming back at me, all I can do is sit there staring at it speechless. I know blades intimately, and I know that this is one of the finest blades I've ever seen. The firm callouses on her hands attest to the time and dedication that went into crafting this work of deadly art and beauty.

Sheathing the blade, I pick up the business card from the bottom of the box. Seeing the address makes my heart clench. Now I know where she is. I shouldn't know that information. What we had is over. I should rip it up and burn it. Erase it from my memory to keep myself and my enemies away from her and her family. Keeping it would be like painting a target on her back if our enemies ever caught wind of her.

My fingers refuse to even bend the card as they brush back and forth over her name. A name that fits the woman so perfectly there is no doubt that God laid his hand over her from the beginning. Damn she was basically made for me but I can't keep her. Too many sharks are in the waters and it isn't safe to bring any new blood into the fold. The best way to keep her safe is to let her go.

Pulling my wallet out, I stuff the card in before loosening my belt to house my new blade. Its weight hangs warmly against my skin just as its maker fit to my side as if she was made to remain there from the start. The handle presses into my lower rib but not so much that it is uncomfortable. No more like a constant presence that gives meaning to our mission. A living reminder of why we are trying so hard to burn their nasty disease from the world.

Shifting the vehicle into drive I make my way out of the small city to head north. The hours and miles past by in silence as I let the images of her filter through my mind's eyes. My last pure ties to the woman before they are tainted by the passing of time. Looking into the clear blue skies I let her name pass over my lips for the last time in a prayer, "Father protect the woman and give her all the happiness in the world that I cannot. Make her days bright and her nights peaceful. Amen. Be well Ember."

Chapter 11

A few miles from home, I battle away another round of tears. A few make it past my lids, and I pull my shirt up to wipe them away. His smell fills my nose, and I clutch the shirt to my chest as insignificant details suddenly filter through my mind.

I don't remember my shirt being this huge or soft on me! Looking down, I realize it isn't my shirt. How the hell did I get all the way home without noticing that somehow, I was wearing his shirt instead of my own?

Quickly, I pull over and stop before pulling it off as I reach for one of my own. There is no way I'm walking into the house wearing a man's shirt. I'd never hear the end of it. Before putting it in my bag, I bury my face in its folds. His spicy scent floods my lungs as I drag in deep breaths as my gut clenches in warm anticipation. God, the man smells so good.

Closing my eyes, I press my lips and put the shirt in my bag. I need to get a grip. My body is reacting worse than when I had to watch Jackson walk towards the plane that would take him around the world. Every time neither of us knew if we would ever see each other again. Both of us refused to even speak of it.

Mikhail isn't mine. We agreed to only the two nights that are now over. I should be hoping to never see the man again, but my traitorous heart is still breaking in my chest.

"Enough!" My yell rings loud over the radio. Shaking my head, I force the man out of my thoughts as I grip the wheel harder.

Merging onto the blacktop again, I skirt the edge of town. Taking a left, I hit gravel as I made my way deeper into the mountain. Finally, with a final right, I hit our driveway and begin the steep climb. The corner of the house comes into view as I wipe another tear away before I smile seeing the kids playing in the snow.

Their faces light up and shrieks of joy fill the air as I park and climb out of the cab. "Mommy!" Josey's little body launches itself into the air, forcing me to jump forward forcing me to catch her so that she doesn't slam face down on the snowy ground.

"Hey, baby girl," I whisper, pulling her close to take in her sweet scent. "Get over here, young man." My fingers wiggle behind my daughter's back, beckoning my boy forward.

"Hunter, we need to get going," I yell up the stairs. "You're gonna make us late."

"I can't find my backpack!" His voice is bordering on outright meltdown.

"Oh, good grief, young man. You can find a trap we laid three weeks ago but not the bag you had five minutes ago." I look over at the hutch, trying to stop my irritation because he left it down here not even five minutes ago. "It's on the hutch where you left it."

I swear the stairs shake as he runs down them before grabbing said bag from where he left it. "Ok, I'm ready."

Mom laughs from the sofa while I shake my head watching him run out the door to the truck where his sister is already waiting. I wrap my arms around her in a quick hug before heading out myself.

"Can I go out with you this weekend?" Hunter turns pleading eyes my way before we're even out of the driveway.

"It's Josey's turn, buddy."

"Rachel asked me to have a sleepover, so you can take Hunter, Mommy." Those bright hazel eyes bubble with so much excitement she bounces in her seat. "Grammy said I could go."

"Next time ask me first, ok? I was looking forward to spending time with you." I will not cry, I promise myself. My little girl is growing up, and I'm not always going to be first in her world. She needs her own friends and interests. God, I hope she skips the emo phase.

"Ok, mommy." Her father's dimple pops as she grins up at me. Since Harrisburg, the sight of Jack in the kids doesn't hurt my heart as much as it used to. I can still breathe instead of nearly crumbling in the pain of never seeing him again in this life.

After dropping the kids off at school, I make my way down to the shop. A face flashes at the end of the porch. They're gone before I can get a good look at their face. I swear I've seen them before but not of someone who should be in my town. I can't tell where I know them from. For now, I push it to the back of my mind.

Dad's behind the counter with Mr. Clansey, going over the new blade he's here to pick up. The clang of the old bell announces my arrival.

"Morning, Ember." Dad waves without taking his eyes off the blade in Clansey's hands, waiting to see if anything isn't what he wants.

"Mornin' dad. What do you think of the blade, Mr. Clansey?" I step behind the glass to stand beside Dad.

The balding gray hair bobs up and down as he continues running critical eyes over my work, looking for any imperfections. The man has ordered a new blade every few months for the past four years like clockwork but still treats each blade as if it's the first one I've forged for him. With a final grunt, he straightens, pulling the glasses off his nose and looking me square in the eye. Another thing he does every time.

"Good." He nods reaching into his pocket and slides the cash into my hand.

"Glad it meets your expectations, sir." I smile, taking the bills and putting them in the register without counting them. The price is always set when he orders, and not once has he found anything not to his liking, not that he'll give me more than a grunt of good in response to the work.

"We'll see you next time then." I hand him the sheath in its box. Another grunt reaches us as he turns and heads out the door.

"If that man didn't buy so many knives from me, I'd be worried that he even liked my work," I joke after the door closes.

"A man of few words', little girl." His hand lands on my shoulder. "Kinda like your old man. He knows quality works when he sees it."

"At least we know he's creating a collection for each of his four grandsons, or I'd be worried where my work ends up."

"Military men want the best equipment." He cracks his neck as the door opens again, letting Adam Leery in.

"I'm gonna get working on the Steven's order," I grumble heading for the back room to get away from the idiot that just came in.

"I need it done by closing," Dad growls in irritation as he watches the man's smile drop when I make myself scarce before the blonde idiot can call my name.

As soon as the door clicks behind me, I turn on the grinder before pulling out the basket marked for the order that doesn't need to be finished for another four days.

Leery doesn't have to know that. Since he moved back into the area two years ago, he's been bent on asking me out. He had an unhealthy crush on me all through school. No matter that I was already with Jack since sixth grade or that he took countless beatings from both my brother and Jack when he didn't know how to back off.

After the fight at our senior prom, I hoped to never see the man again. Just my luck he would move back after his divorce. Maggie adored Adam from the beginning, but to him she was always second best. Poor girl deserves a hell of a lot better. After she caught him cheating for the tenth time, she finally wised up and kicked him out of their Williamsport home.

Just the feeling of him in the same building as me makes me feel sick. Where's a big bad Russian when I need one? My core clenches, picturing Mikhail walking in to stand behind me, folding his arms with a scowl on his face as Adam tries to weasel his way into my life yet again.

He'd probably make him piss himself trying to get out the door. I'm still grinning like a fool when Dad walks back to let me know Adam's gone. I smile at him as he shakes his head before going back to the front.

Chapter 12

Music blasts through the floor of the club as I make my way across the room toward our back office. Vlad's personal guard nods at me as I head in and close the door behind me.

One quick touch to the panel reveals the password key. The barest click sounds as the bookcase swings forward. Thirty steps down, and I walk into the room with my oldest brothers. Vlad sits at his desk leaning back without any visible emotion.

Dimitri sits with his hip perched on the dark cherry wood with a grin lighting up his entire face. Neither spares me a glance as they focus wholeheartedly on the man kneeling on the cement in chains.

"Pakhan." I make sure to use his position when speaking to my brother today. He nods at me at the same time he leans forward, and Dimitri's low rumble of laughter fills the room.

Rolling my jacket from my shoulders, I hang it by the door as I start rolling the shelves of my shirt. The dark swirls of my tattoos slowly come to light, making the man on the floor shake in fear before he finds his spine and sits up straighter. Like a good Russian soldier he will face his death with a brave face but the fear still bleeds out of his pores like a sickness. He knows what is about to happen and the fact that I am the one to deliver it has him praying for strength. If I walk through someone's door they know that they will never walk out again.

Good. I want his fear. The demons in me feed off of it. Letting the demons wake, I chuckle darkly as I squat down invading the little fucker's personal space. The demons spread my lips in sadistic glee as they take him in.

We aren't here to play nice but play we will. The man on the floor is a rat. What my brother and the head of the family wants is answers, and I am who he sends for when he needs to get them. Given what this man has been through with the family blood is the only option for his sins.

"If you wanted my attention, Anton, all you had to do was say so." Without waiting for a come back, I slam my fist into his already bruised face.

"Now that we've said our greeting, how about you tell me what you have to say." I grab the short sweaty brown hair to pull him back to meet my fist again.

70

Blood starts pouring from his nose before he coughs and a few wet wads land at my feet. "I don't have anything more to say to you than I had to the Pakhan. I was framed. You know I would never go against the family." He glares back at me but I see the hint of worry in his eyes.

"Yes, everyone is always innocent, aren't they, Dimitri?"

"Yes, so innocent, brother." He laughs as he gets up and casually walks into my area. "Yes, such an innocent man that when our Pakhan showed up to simply talk about why our numbers aren't adding up, he destroyed all of his systems to keep us in the dark."

"That doesn't sound like an innocent man to me." I shake my head in mock pity before leaning closer to the rat. "What do you think, Anton, doesn't that sound like an innocent man's actions to you?"

Before he can speak, my fist connects with his face again. I grin as he steadies himself before spitting blood on my face. Chuckling I don't bother wiping it off when more will only be added shortly. Reaching to my waist, I pull out my new knife. The sharp blade gleams under the bright light as I bring it to my eye level. The contrasting metals make the knife look just as beautiful as it is deadly.

I'm sure Ember never intended for her work to be used in such a fashion. She couldn't know what dangers lay in the daily dealings of my life but it would be a shame to let such work go to waste by letting it sit. The tang is much larger than my normal ones and ten times sharper. My knife skills are well known in our world, and I smile even more when his eyes widen.

"Beautiful, isn't it? In all my years I've never found one so perfect." A flick of my wrist opens a line just under his eye.

He tries to hold in his screams as each cut becomes longer,

71

wider, and deeper. After an hour, he sits shivering in his chains, tears pouring from his eyes, whimpering but still refusing to tell us what we want to know. So begins another hour of plying my knife on the trash before me.

"Are you ready to speak?" Blood soaks my shirt and hands as I grin down at him before cutting off another finger.

When he doesn't say anything, I reach into my breast pocket and pull out what I have to show him next. "I wonder what dear Sofia would think if she knew about your weekly visits to your second family? What about Nora? Does she know about your wife and kids?"

"You won't touch my children." He sits taller with a tired grin. "Everyone knows you would never cross that rule."

Vlad tosses Dimitri a tablet. Leaning down, my brother shows him the screen. Sofia and her two children play in their yard. The sound of their laughter bounces off the walls.

Anton pales but doesn't speak until Dimitri taps a few keys splitting the screen to show Nora sitting in her nursery rocking her two-month-old son. Another tap shows an aerial view of both houses each with a group of five men waiting for my brother's command.

Anton shakes but doesn't cry. "Go to Hell." His words come out in a whisper unable to tear his eyes from the images.

Vlad lifts his phone with dead eyes. "Do it."

Screams fill the room from the tablet as Anton strains against the metal. "You bastards! I'll kill you all!" He curls into himself as he sobs. "They are going to kill you. I'm not the only one." He starts laughing. He bites something in his teeth seconds before he starts foaming at the mouth.

We all jump to pry his mouth open. There is nothing any of us can do. The last nerve endings in his body twitch before going still. Sighing, I stand and change into clean clothes, tossing my bloody ones into the black bag sitting by the door. One of us will burn them shortly.

Dimitri curses as he tosses the tablet onto the desk. "Pathetic fool."

Vlad calmly stands and makes his way back up as we follow him. We close the entrance before everyone sits down.

My oldest brother nods, and the door is opened, allowing Sofia and Nora into the room. "Thank you for coming to me, but he killed himself before he could tell us anything of value."

"He played both of us, Pakhan." Sofia raises her head as she and Nora share a smile. "But he did give us each other to lean on. Our children will be safer now."

"What kind of man would sell off his own family?" Dimitri grumbles in disgust.

"A sick one." Nora's voice is soft but full of steel. "One who needed to be put down."

Chapter 13

Slamming the door of my car, I hit the lock button and stalk toward the inner office of the old fading red brick warehouse that we use as a cover for operations. I pass rooms full of men welding and building things without acknowledging any of them or they me. Every one of them works for the family.

Pressing my hand to the scanner, I enter my code before hearing the click and pushing my way in. I'm angry and irritated, wanting nothing more than to throw myself in the chair. Only a lifetime of holding myself calm and collected on the outside allows me to sink into the seat with the dignity demanded of a prominent member of the bratva.

"Tell me you finally found something," I demand from the figure at the other end of the table. Aside from my own men in the room are five of the freelance group we work with as well as their leader.

We keep our numbers small in our time with them to limit what they know of our dealings. I wish I could say they were stupid to what we are, but they aren't in exchange for working with them they turn a blind eye to the less legal business we do in our city.

Viking picks up a file, sliding it down the table to me. "This came in just last night. We checked all channels and found that it was legit." His body stays tense in his seat. I've never seen him so amped up before. He's been nothing but calm and cool since the moment he joined our joint force. Seeing him on edge raises my own unease.

Opening the file, I start reading. Less than a sentence in and my body in wound as tight as Viking's. Emporium Pennsylvania. That's where Ember lives.

Flashes of her spread out beneath me race through my mind before I shut them down. My brain races praying it isn't what I think it is. The more I read the surer I am that my dread is well-founded.

"No name on the target?" I ask looking up hoping for good news.

"Nothing." He shakes his head. "I'll be leading in tandem with you on this one. I grew up there. It isn't a place to run around without knowing the land. Too many old mines, cliffs, and drop-offs. Locals are closed off most of the year and dislike outsiders. My team's ready to go wheels up in two hours then it's a twenty-minute drive from the airport into the town. We split into two teams I'll take the center of town you stay near the edge."

My jaw tenses as I shake my head. My gut tells me waiting will cost us. We don't have two hours.

"We've wasted enough time on these bastards. I want this group dealt with." My knuckles crack harshly thinking how many times we got there too late to kill the dirty bastards. "An hour too quick for you and your men?" I asked Viking.

"We'll be ready." He's as angry as I am at our repeated failure to take down these kidnapping-slaving bastards.

Everyone stands to change and heads out to grab their gear. A quick press of an encoded app signals to my family that I'm going dark before leaving it in a coated locker to block unwanted searches.

Swiftly I gear myself up and head for the airfield. I'm the first one there besides the pilot rushing around to get the bird ready for our rushed flight. I nod at each man as they arrive and load into the helicopter.

Viking and I are the last to load up before the door is slammed shut. Ear phones settle in place to block out the loud sounds of the bird as it lifts into the air. Our city falls away below us as Irish directs us to the west and the up coming mission. Dear Father, please keep her safe if she is the one in danger. Let us get there in time to save who ever is in trouble at this time. Amen I finish silently.

Chapter 14

The trap line is kicking off the year decently. I smile as I think of all the skins that need to be cured in the back of the truck as I head home from the cabin. The kids are running from the door shouting for me before I'm even stopped.

Opening my door, they tackled me nearly knocking me to the snow-covered muddy ground. Wrapping them in my arms I stand up clutching them tightly. Lord, I have missed these two. With some quick adjustments, I get us up the slippery steps and into the house without dropping or landing on anyone.

"Grammy's making venison stew for supper tonight!" The kids grin at me.

"Sounds delicious. Go grab your coats." I grin back, setting them both down as I make my way to the kitchen to hug Mom. "I'm going to get the kids out of your hair for a few hours to help me in the shop. We'll be back in time for dinner."

"Sounds good, honey." She kisses my cheek before going back to chunking up the meat. "Your dad's out back playing with that dang old truck again." She rolls her eyes as she gives me a small smile. "Oh, there's a letter from Della and Kenna on the fridge for you."

I grin pulling it off and shove it into the pocket of my coat eager to open it but wanting to do us in private. "I'll read it at the shop."

"Make sure you send our love when you write back."

Laughing, I head for the door as the kids pull on their gloves. Heading to the truck we hear my dad grumble under the hood of the truck behind the house. Dad bought that old bucket of bolts when Joey and Jackson left for their first deployment. It's sad to see him working on it by himself over the years.

Whenever Jackson and my brother found time to come home from which ever base we were stationed at, the guys always went out together to work on it. I know Dad should have finished it years ago but stubbornly he holds out on fixing it in the hopes that someday soon Joe will walk through the door so they can do it together like they agreed to. Smiling bitterly, I send up a silent prayer that my brother is safe wherever he is.

I spend the next half hour singing with the kids till we reached our storefront. Most shops already have their lights off and are home for supper. The bar is still lively with music filling the few buildings around us. Everything is quiet and simple as it always is when the tourists aren't in town. Unlocking the door, we slip in, lock it, and get to work in the back cleaning everything up.

The new hides are sorted,wrapped, and put in the freezer till I'm ready to deal with them. I'll have to go to the After an hour we finish, and I get out pieces of scrape leather for the kids to play with as I work on a sheath for a knife that I just finished before I left to check the line.

Remembering the letter, I pulled it out and read it with a smile on my face. Getting to see what is happening in my friends lives, never fails to put me in a good mood. People who thought I was backward would never be able to handle Della. She was even more of a recluse than I am. Living on horse back year round she stays in the mountains and away from people as much as possible.

The only time she left the mountains was for the fur sale which is where we met. Back then all Dad and I did was trap and sell the furs. When I found her table and saw the blade work that she did by hand I was impressed. If we wouldn't have been surrounded by a room full of other buyers we would have talked for hours. So we did the logical next best thing and met up after the event ended.

Working with metal is something that I have always enjoyed watching but had no clue how to do. Our town is small and isolated because of the harshness of the weather and terrain. You don't live here and love it without wanting every challenge the place throws your way. We were barely making the bills on the military salary and I needed a new way to bring in money. After so wheeling and dealing she finally agreed to take me out and teach me.

This land will chew you up and spit you out. It makes for a

hard life and hard people. Jackson and I had only left because of his duty stations but we always planned to return a grow our family to our hometown. With the new skills we would be able to live comfortably on what we could make off the land.

After meeting Della, I spent six months in the remote mountains of Idaho learning from her while Jackson was on his first deployment and only went back to my base housing when my pregnant ass couldn't keep up with her across the rugged terrain.

That time was invaluable though. She taught me how to tamper and bend steel, how to carve antlers, and how to work intricate designs into leather. The success I had today was all thanks to her. I miss the freedom of living off the land the way she does.

That's where I also met Kenna or as Della, and I liked to call her crazy Kenna. I swear that woman has more energy than I've ever seen and when she decides on something no one is going to talk her out of it. Out of the three of us, she is never going to settle down. She also lost family overseas and used that as motivation to open an equine therapy center and retreat for all military no matter what.

On a trip into town, we ran into Leah and her daughter Mazie. Kenna and Della are great with horses and the food Leah can make over an open fire is next level. They are part of a search and rescue team when Idaho and Montana need help getting into places no one else would dare to go.

My home mountains have nothing on places they regularly get into. I'm so proud of how far the women I view as sisters have come and accomplished.

My body vibrates with the need to be out there with them again. I miss them so much. It's been a few years since we've all been together and with the way things are looking the chances are good, I'll be able to head out to see them soon.

Shaking the thoughts from my head, I pick up a needle and sinew to stitch the two halves lined with glue together to create a strong seal. The customer didn't want anything etched into the leather, just a simple sheath for the skinning knife I made.

The motions of the stitching are automatic letting my mind wander. Blue eyes flash at me as strong hands twist my body around. Husky Russian words breathe across the back of my neck leaving me hot and aroused. Damn, it's been months since that day, and it still feels as real as in that moment.

The bell over the door ringing brings me back to the present. Leaving my work on the table, I get up and step into the front of the store. Hints of danger flicker across my awareness but I keep a calm front as I take in the individuals before me.

"We aren't open right now gentleman. You'll have to come back tomorrow," I say to the three men as they spread out in front of me. A fourth leans over the display cases to my right.

"I don't think so, honey." A voice purrs in my ear as metal presses into the side of my head and my whole body freezes. The cold steel traces over my cheek and harshly, digging the sight into skin. A thin line of blood seeps to the surface but still I don't react. I have to time everything right if I'm going to keep the kids safe.

"Leave my mom alone!"

Oh God no. "Run, Hunter!"

Chapter 15

The flight is too long and not long enough in the same breath. I pray that my gut is wrong and the group we're after aren't hunting the woman who's occupied my mind nonstop for the past two months. The men are unusually quiet as we hop into the trucks waiting for us at the small airfield.

"Don't rely on compasses here they won't work. Too much iron ore in the mountains." Viking reminds us. "Stay off comms unless needed we don't want to draw attention to ourselves."

My hand tightens on the wheel as we split up on the edge of

town. Damn I knew this wasn't a big town, but it shocks me how small and isolated it is. Not as bad as some places I've been to back in Russia but for the U.S. it feels like a different country. All the shops but the bar is closed as we drive slowly by. A few patrons eye us cautiously but are quick to dismiss our presence.

My gut tenses as I slowly drive past the shop where Ember works. All the lights are on in the back and the sign says closed, but the door is standing open. Frowning I roll to a stop taking in all the tall tale signs in front of me as my mind races. Something is off. I send another quick prayer that I'm wrongs before getting out.

"Mikhail," Ilya says eyes clocking all the things out of place that mine are.

"I know." Casually I hop out and make my way to the open door. With each step, my gut tells me that something is wrong. My eyes scan the street surrounding the shop before detailing everything on the other side of the glass.

A small bell hangs at the top of the door. Shooting a look at Ilya I wait for him to disappear around the back of the building before slipping into the shop as well. I clock the broken glass and knives scattered around the floor as I step around the worst of it. Displays lay in ruin, the register is busted open, and blood spots fan over the wooden floor. My heart drops lower in my gut with each new sign of struggle.

Ilya and I regroup at the door separating the two areas of the shop. We each take stock of the separate rooms. Most of the damage is only in the front but a broken chair and thrown tools littler this room as well. Two coats are flung to different sides of the area. Rage roars through me as I take in the mess.

They had her! I'm so angry that I nearly miss the first soft noise from the cupboards on the back wall. Ilya and I both raise our guns as we stalk closer. We each take a side as he reaches down and yanks the door open. The tip of our weapons waver at the sight that greets us.

A little girl no more than five, huddles shaking in the darkness making my breath seize in my lungs as she cries sinking as far back as she can. Aside from the darker hair, she's the perfect likeness to Ember. There's no doubt in my mind who she belongs to. The tears in her eyes nearly break my already pounding heart. We can't be too late.

"Hello, Milaya." I crouch down slipping my gun back into the holster. "My name is Mikhail. I'm a friend of your mother's. Are you hurt anywhere?" I soften my tone not wanting to scare her any further as I motioning for Ilya to back up.

She sniffs holding a familiar denim fleece jacket much too large for her tighter to her chest. "How do I know you know my mommy?"

"Good girl." I praise pride bubbling up that she won't trust so easily. Reaching down I pull the blade on my hip free to show her mother's work.

"Your mommy gave this to me when we met in Harrisburg. It's alright Milaya my friends and I are going to find her, but we want to make sure you're ok first. Can you come out?" I reach out my hand for her after rehoming the knife.

"Hunter said to stay here and be quiet." Her little lip trembles in uncertainty but she holds my eyes just like her mother.

"Who is Hunter?" Red fills my eyes at the mention of another man. Damn it, I need to calm down before I give this little one a reason to fear me.

"My brother. He told me to hide here and then he went to help mommy. There was a fight. I heard the bad men take him and Mommy."

My guts release and contract at her confession. A son. Not another man. Relief and fear roll through me leaving a sour taste in my mouth. Not only has Ember been taken but also her son. This situation just keeps getting worse. This group has no complaints about putting women and children through hell. We need to move or we will lose them.

"And you did so good, Milaya but you can come out now so we can get you somewhere safe before we go after them." I reach out with my other hand hoping she will come out by herself.

"That's not my name." She gives an angry pout as she holds back more tears. She hugs the jacket tighter and refuses to move. Damn she's just like her mother. I can't help the smile that lifts my lips.

Ilya coughs to cover his laugh as the rest of our team joins us but they stay back without saying anything. They will wait for me to give them the all clear before coming in.

"I know." I give a chuckle of my own because dang it she has her mother's sass. "Milaya means precious in my home country. I promise none of us will hurt you."

Her eyes dart around the room, taking in the men standing back before scooting forward and lifting her arms up to me. Gently I wrap my hands around her small frame and pull her into my arms. The moment her small weight settles against me, my heart knocks against my ribs in a few erratic beats before settling into a strong beat. My most terrifying demons lift their heads but instead of demanding pain they want to protect. Fuck this isn't good.

Cupping the back of her head I stand and close my eyes for a moment to get them under control. It feels like a piece of me was missing and I didn't know it. "Good girl, Milaya," I say shifting her so I can support her legs in their attempt to curl around my waist and her head tucking itself under my chin.

The sound of Viking's curses fills the front of the store as we turn to meet him. "What the Hell happ……." His words die as he notices the child in my arms.

I see his lips move in a silent no as he shakes his head. He quickly gathers himself before coming to stand in front of me, a hand raised and extended towards the child in my arms.

Growling, I step back holding her more tightly to myself. Protective urges surge to the front as I glare at the man I've worked with for the last five years. I don't want him touching Ember's child and neither do my demons. They are ready to fight anyone over her.

I often care for the little ones we rescue, but I've never snapped at anyone from our team for trying to come near one of them before. For this child, I would rip apart the world before I let anything, or anyone touch her.

He shot me a questioning look before dropping his arm. His voice comes out rough as he looks at her hazel eyes pecking at him through my arms. "What's your name sweetheart?"

Her little arms cling tighter to my neck. "Josey."

"What's your last name?" Looking as if he already knows what she's going to say he pulls himself up straighter.

"Russell."

For a moment I'm worried the man might drop to his knees from the range of pain that flashes in his eyes. He recovers quickly, giving her a small nearly teary smile. "How about we get you back home then? I'm sure your grandparents are worried about you." He turns to give me a look that has my gut clenching.

"What about Mommy and Hunter?"

I answer before he can. "We'll get them Milaya. I promise."

She searches my eyes with the same intensity as her mother did all those months ago in the confines of the elevator. With a nod, she rests her head on my shoulder as we make our way out to the trucks.

"Mustang, Tip, Hatch you're with us," Viking growls getting into his truck. "The rest of you." He stops giving everyone a nod which they return before heading out to look for clues. My men don't need my instructions before drifting off to sweep the area as well.

Climbing into the passenger seat, I end up holding Josey when she refuses to be set down. The men and I share a look before letting her have her way. I smile stroking her hair as I remember her mother clinging to me as well. The guys sit in the back without a word as we head out of town.

"How do you know where I live?" Josey pecks over at the big man beside us.

He turns to her with a soft smile. "I grew up here. Your mommy and I go way back."

I force the growl threatening to erupt back down as I glare at him. I hate what he is implying about him and Ember. The thought of another man near her makes me want to kill someone. Only little Josey still sitting in my lap keeps the beast at bay. The rest of the thirty-minute drive is silent, which I'm thankful for.

Parking the truck, we leave Mustang, Tip, and Hatch to watch our back as we head for the door. Instead of knocking like I expect Viking walks right in as if he owns the place. Heading through a mudroom he turns right into what I would call the living room.

A woman sits on the couch knitting needles frozen in place

as she looks at us with wide eyes. Her grey eyes tear up as she takes in the man in front of me. Snatching the hat from his head, Viking steps forward twisting it in his hands with his head bowed. "Momma."

I swear the floor nearly falls away from me as she sobs. Throwing her knitting down to rush to him nearly falling in her haste to grab him. I hug Josey closer to me as I watch the big man fall into her arms stunned at this newest revelation. I'd fucked Viking's sister not once, not twice but multiple times.

God help me because when we found her, I don't think I will be able to stop the possessiveness I feel toward her. It would be better if I did that but do, I really want to? Can I let her go a second time when I barely held myself back the first time. And that was before I held her daughter in my arms. What kind of bastard did that make me?

"Charlie!" The woman calls still holding Viking close as her hands run over his rough checks. "Charlie, come out here now!"

My gut meets the floor again as an older version of Viking walks into the room. The man only looks old because of the gray hair and years of wisdom in his hazel eyes. His body is all muscle despite his late years. His eyes lock on Viking as he comes to a sudden stop, his big hands gripping a shotgun.

"Joe." The man sets the gun against the wall before gripping Viking's neck to pull him into a hug.

"Son," his voice breaks with raw emotions. "I knew you were out there. We've missed you, boy. Wait till your sister sees you."

Chapter 16

Men cursing and my body being thrown about in the back seat of a car finally pull my aching mind from the numb darkness. The pain hammering in my skull makes me groan when I try to open my eyes. Thankfully the darkness of the storm clouds have taken what little light is left so my eyes aren't effected to much by the light.

My heart nearly stops as my mind catches up with my current situation. Strange guys were coming into the shop, a gun pressed against my head. Hunter yelling for them to leave me alone as he charged them. One of them grabbed my son as I launched myself at them to get to my son, yelling for him to run.

"Mom." Little hands grab hold of my shirt as I slide on another turn. The attempt doesn't doesn't stop me from slamming into the door. Damn that hurt.

Prying my eyes open, I ignore the pain and push the nausea away. I have to see that he isn't hurt. "Baby."

He sits above me buckled in watching me with scared hazel eyes. His chestnut brown hair is a mess laying around on his swollen cheek. Other than the swelling he doesn't seem to be hurt and it seem fills me with rage that someone touched my child.

"You, ok?" He nods, easing some of my fears.

"I'm sorry Mom."

I open my mouth to tell him it's not his fault, but someone turns around pushing him into the seat with force. He whimpers when the arm doesn't let go right away.

"Shut your mouth brat," the man spits at him. Then his eyes turn down to me and he grins. "You just lay there and be quiet so we won't have to get rough again."

I glare up at him as best I can with the pain in my head, but I hold my tongue to keep the words inside. For now, I'll wait and gather my strength. Soon they will make a mistake and then they will pay. Hunter's hand grips me tighter as the man grins back at us, but I refuse to be the first to look away.

"Oh, good you're going to fight." He laughs stroking a finger down my cheek before turning around as the driver curses harshly and the vehicle comes to a sliding stop.

"Is foolish to keep going in this weather!" A hand slams into the dash. "We need to find a place to wait it out." Their thick accents remind me of Mikhail but seem different at the same time. The sound is harsher and the words don't sound the same.

The man turns back to me again as he pulls a gun and levels it on my son. "Here's how it's going to be, little mamma." the gun cocks. "We need a place to stop, and you're going to tell us what's down this road."

Reaching down he pulls my limp body up. I lock eyes with Hunter, willing him to be strong. "Now, don't look at him, mamma, look at the road." He laughs and shakes me.

I stare through the falling snow for a minute till I spot familiar trees and boulders. "Hunter shack five hundred yards west," I say not fighting him. The longer we stay in the mountains the better our chances.

"See not so hard." He smiles trailing his finger down my cheek again before delivering a stinging slap. The nasty feelings his touch invokes clear my mind and I know who has us. The man who hit on me in Harrisburg. I keep my face void of emotion. "Have to leave the car cross the bridge and follow the footpath."

There's no big Russian to help me this time but that's okay. They stupidly brought me to my hunting grounds. I'll make sure they don't leave here alive. I just have to get Hunter away to safety, and then I can have fun. The thought makes me giddy, but I keep my face blank.

It takes him a minute to see what I mean, and he isn't happy about it. There's no way a vehicle can cross the small bridge. Getting out he rips the door open and pulls me out, dropping me into the fresh snow. Hissing I hold in the groan of pain as he pulls Hunter out next.

"Get up now," he demands, gun against my child again. He dies first. Both the devil and the angel on my shoulders agree on that.

Pushing the pain aside, I stand, swaying for a moment before steadying myself. We wait for the others to gather before he pushes me ahead to make me lead the way.

The air whips around me as the storm worsens, but I barely feel the wind through my sweater as anger heats my blood. With each step, my feet grow stronger as I lead them over the old bridge and start up a slick shale path toward old man Dillard's rundown cabin.

The only reassuring thing I can find in this mess is that Josey isn't with us. Hunter must have hidden her before trying to fight the men at the shop. If we weren't home by supper, mom would call the shop to find out why. We were never late without a call. She'd be found very soon.

I didn't need a big bad Russian man to help me out of this mess. I had years to learn this land and more military uncles than I could shake a stick at. As long as I keep my head, none of these bastards will be seen again.

"I'm going to enjoy breaking you when we get out of this god-forsaken place." He leans into my side pushing me to my knees as he stands leering down at me with the same nasty smile. "Yes, that's a good look for you." He laughs pushing me forward again.

"Enough Vin," another man snaps behind him. "If you hadn't fucked up the first time we wouldn't be here." He grabs Hunter by the coat pushing him ahead of us.

Vin grabs me pushing me ahead of him. "Don't worry I'll make sure your spawn is sold to the worst man I know." He laughs slapping my ass hard.

I try to ignore all the things he hopes happen to Hunter but with each word out of his mouth, it gets harder and harder to remain unaffected. His hand makes contact with my ass again so hard that I almost lose my footing and fall.

"Touch me again and you're a dead man," I growl in warning before I can stop myself.

His head falls back as he roars in laughter. "That dirty Bratva bastard isn't around to save you this time. Don't worry before it's over I'll let him see you one last time. Tie him up, make him bleed, and let him watch as I make you scream. Maybe I'll kill him quickly if you ask me real nicely before I fuck you as his blood drains."

He grabs my hair jerking my head back and mashing his lips against mine. All thoughts of playing nice fly from my mind as I head butt the asshole making him stumble back.

"Not if I kill you first." I hiss barreling into him sending us in a tumble of flailing limbs down the hundred-foot slick cliff. A pile of boulders stops our fall halfway down. Pain lances alone the entire length of my ribs, but I push it away as I get back to my feet.

"You stupid little bitch," he growls trying to get up to look for his fallen gun in the rocks. He stumbles in the mud and slush as several rocks give way under his feet.

I'm on him again driving him into the stone. Grabbing a fist-sized rock, I swing for his head. He barely ducks under the edge of it with a curse. Kicking his leg from under him I swung again smashing the hard edge into his shoulder. The impact feels great as it vibrates my hand.

Screaming in pain, he grabs his arm and tries to clumsily, roll away from me. He gets on the other side of the rocks, and I jump over them after him. Feet slipping in the snow without purchase gives me the opening I need. I swing with every ounce of strength I have left. A mist of crimson spray blankets the snow and I lift the rock to let it fall one more time.

Just as the rock starts its downward fall, a pistol shot cracks through the air. Searing pain slams into the back of my shoulder, sending me backward in an uncontrolled roll toward the bottom and into the rushing creek.

Hunter's scream for me echoes above before the water rushes over me. I'm not going out like this. This is not how it ends. They haven't seen the last of me. Hunter needs me. I will kill every one of the bastards who dared touch mine.

Chapter 17

We dropped Josey off with her grandparents an hour ago. The team asked around town and was lucky enough that a man at the bar had seen two black out-of-state SUVs head west out of town. Good old small towners and their inability to stay out of other people's business.

We regroup and head out, each of us more determined to catch them than before. Everyone had seen Viking's, reaction to Josey and made the connection on their own. Now this is personal for us. We are now fighting to find and protect one of our own. The storm the Irish warned us about soon hits, adding to the slushy snow already on the ground.

Viking has me stay in his truck as the others trail behind us. I banished any thoughts but finding Ember and her son. Alive is all I will allow myself to think about. "This is normal weather," I ask frowning as the wind picks up, working its way toward a whiteout.

"No," he growls counter steering as we slide on another patch of unseen ice. "We have to stop. I can't see shit." His fist pounds the wheel in anger.

"We turning back?" Mustang breaks his silence with gritted teeth as the ass end twists too close to the end for comfort.

Instead of answering, Viking turns right onto a track that barely fits the truck. The number of potholes we roll over without knowing has everyone bracing themselves or risk being thrown into the roof.

None of us are willing to speak and bite our tongue. Thankfully, after two miles he stops in front of a small creek.

"Let's go." He jumps out.

"How far." I raise my voice to be heard over the screaming wind.

"1000 yards up," he yells back pointing up the thick tree-covered ridge. All our men are grim-faced but don't say a word as they file after Viking over the small footbridge.

Ilya and I cover our rear as we slowly make our way up the switchback trail. If it weren't for our training, I'm sure half of us would end up in the creek below. The increasing snow makes the numerous rocks slick forcing a much slower pace. Even with the many trees and brush don't do much to help us as we go. Whoever owns this cabin is in incredible shape. Dear

Father get us up this slope in one piece, Amen.

After half an hour of fighting our way up the slope, Viking stops us under a rock overhang that will allow all of our group to sit comfortably out of the weather. Stacked rock encloses the area creating a large blind. A large two-foot-thick log sits close to the wall, the top rubbed smooth from constant use. Against the back of the overhang is a ring of stones blackened from a fire.

Everyone sits except for Viking and I as we stand on either side of the entrance scanning the land around us to the best of our ability in the swirling snow. Leaning against the stone, I grip the rounded handle of the knife Ember gave me as I pray that we find her safe. I was a fool to let her go the way I did in Harrisburg. Her memory haunts me every night, leaving me frustrated all day long. Now that I am so close to holding her again, I learn who her family is.

It's going to be a shit show anyway I go about it. Should I allow the threat of her brother's wrath keep me from being with the only woman I can't keep out of my mind? My eyes flick to Viking before watching the mounting snow again. He's a good man and a good partner to have your back, even if we were not always on the same side of the law.

We'd become close over the countless jobs we worked together and though I don't know about him being a friend we both held a healthy respect for each other. Is pursuing his sister worth the risk to our teams? Once he accepts the idea of us I'm sure all of us would be alright.

My body is all for it but now that I have a chance to think I'm not so sure. Could I walk away from this woman? And Josey? That little doll is already in my heart, and all I'd done was hold her for less than an hour. Hell, I'd even been willing to gut her uncle to keep her in my arms. When we left, she rushed to hug me and demanded I bring her mother and brother back. There was no doubt I would do so. Is it right to fight for them or better to simply walk away?

The image of her with another man flashes before me making me feel feral with hostility. My heart and soul both scream out mine with resounding force unwilling to share what they have discovered and claimed. Perhaps a greater question is was Ember willing to risk her current life to be a part of mine? My demons raise up and demand that she is ours no matter what she says.

After a brief rest, we signal for the men to get up so we can continue climbing to the promised shelter above. It takes another hour to reach the top as it becomes even steeper and most of our men are out of breath from the climb. They sigh in relief as we follow Viking through the trees and see a cabin. He makes quick work of pulling a nail-studded board from off the door before moving us into the interior.

The inside is dark as we each pull our mags out, so we don't trip over anything. Viking walks outside again, and we hear a generator fire up before he comes back in and flips a switch lighting up the room. In the light, it's surprising to see that the walls are log and chink. A fifteen-by-thirty-foot area houses a small kitchen with an old cast-iron stove.

Whoever brought that monstrosity of metal up here has my respect and sympathy. I know I'm not motivated enough to attempt it. Open shelves spans the wall above the stove holding canned foods next to a double bed sectioned off by a curtain in one half. Where we stand a small couch and pair of chairs face a large stone fireplace. A loft with beds sits above the kitchen area.

Chapter 17

We get both fires going quickly. As the area warms Viking pulls out pots and food from the shelves and starts cooking. The smell of burger cooking has my mouth watering.

"The people who own this place going to be ok with us being here and using their stuff?" Joker asks, watching everything from a chair by the fire.

"Don't think they're going to have a problem." I chuckle pointing to the pictures lining the walls around the fireplace that I've spent the last ten minutes studying. Fuck my woman is beautiful. Wait. Not my woman I remind myself. Not yet anyway my demons snicker back. No, I can't have her I argue. But I want her and damn it I think I need her.

Everyone looks at the wall and their jaws drop. Joker and Mustang leap out of their seats and press their noses to the wall.

"Holy shit Viking what happened?" Mustang asks with a laugh. "You got ugly man."

We all have a good laugh as Viking flips us off over his shoulder as he stirs whatever is in the pan. "Yeah, have your laugh assholes. Just remember I'll be the one laughing tomorrow as I watch you all bust your asses." We all grin at each other as we sit down to eat. The growing hard ass men that we are nothing is left when we're done.

"I'm the first watch on the west side," I say grabbing my coat and gun before heading outside. I need the time to myself. The photos on the wall keep pulling my eyes more than is safe in Viking's company while I'm unsure of the right direction to take.

Finding a rock with a decent windbreak to hunker down against it as I let my eyes adjust to the darkness. Sweeping the area for any movement and my ears strain to hear any sound over the howling of the wind. Damn the wind is bitter tonight.

Pulling my coat closer I settle in for my shift.

After two hours, my watch is up. My joints are eager for a shift in position. Just before I can move to stand, however, a movement at the edge of the ridge catches my attention. It's there one moment gone the next, so I sit still for several more minutes wondering if I'm seeing things.

About to call myself an idiot I freeze a moment later when I see movement again but closer this time. Tucking my rifle by the rock I pull my blade, roll onto the balls of my feet, and wait as I watch the movement form into a figure. It's closer now allowing me to make out the outline of a person as they stumble closer. The wind dies down for a few minutes giving me a clearer view of the person. I'm so stunned by their identity that I can't stop myself from letting out a shout. How is she here?

"Ember!!" I leap onto my feet and beat it towards her.

She stumbles falling to her knees just as I reach her. Fear has me dropping to my knees beside her as I grab her and pull her into the shelter of my body. The shaking of her form lays limply in my hold making my demons roar for blood.

"Ember," I whisper as I twist her, searching for injuries.

"Detka, what happened? Where is Hunter?" My head jerks up looking for the boy only to find no one else around. Dread fills my blood as my mind whirls with a million possibilities of what could have happened.

Her head rolls against my chest with a low moan. Hazel eyes flutter fighting to stay open at the sound of my voice the color dims instead of the bright strength they usually hold. "Mikhail?"

Her lips tremble already blue from the cold as she weakly reaches for my face. Her icy fingers softly slide over my longer whiskers with a soft smile and her eyes light up just a fraction.

"I miss you. Why do I miss you so much already? I'm so cold, Mikhail. Is it warmer where you are?" Her eyes flutter in an attempt to stay open.

Breathing deeply in an attempt to calm my racing heart I kiss the palm of her hand to show her that I am in fact with her. That I'm real and she's safe but seems to be going into shock. "I've got you, moye malen'koye plamya. I'm right here, krasivyy."

Pushing her tangled and freezing wet hair off her face, I just about stop breathing at the jagged line of blood staining the whole upper right side of her face. I push the fear away and grab her left shoulder to pull her closer so I can lift her. She needs to get out of the storm before she freezes.

Her body tenses under my touch, and a low haunting cry leaves her lips causing me to frantically search with my fingers over her arm. I freeze when they slide in a wet spot. They come away sticky with blood. Fuck! Ripping my jacket off, I wrap her shaking form in it. It's too dark to see how bad it is.

As gently as possible, I lift her trembling body into my arms, cradling her to my chest as I run for the cabin. "Hang on, Ember. Everything will be alright. I promise everything will be alright."

My boot slams into the wood as I yell for someone to open the door. As soon as the seal cracks, I push my way through, heading for the table as Mustang stumbles to right himself from behind the door. I don't wait to see if he stays up as I rush to the table.

"Get me blankets and the kit," I yell at them as I settle her against the wooden top. Now that I have light, I can see her clearly and it shocks me to my core.

She's completely soaked from head-to-toe, ice already clings to her shaking form. Bruising on her jaw, a cut line around her throat, cheek, a large gash on her forehead, and blood dripping from a bullet wound in the back of her shoulder. Guilt and rage roar through my body and it's a struggle to breathe. I try to push it away so I can take care of her.

"Kakogo cherta? Bozhe Moy! Has she been shot?" Ilya asks in shock at my elbow with the quilt from the couch in his hands which he promptly tosses aside to help me look her over.

Ignoring him, I let my training kick in as I set about stripping her of her soaked clothes starting with her boots. Once her boots, pants, and socks are off, Ilya throws a blanket over her and starts rubbing her feet roughly to get her blood flowing. She moans trying to move away from his harsh touch.

Viking appears at my side with more blankets. Seeing his sister shocks him but he doesn't let the fear set in. He sits them on a chair before lifting her so we can get her sweater and thermal off.

Every man in the room pauses at the nasty bruising that lines the span of her whole left side. It looks fresh but already has color reached a dark hue. It looks like she's been thrown down a mountain. He throws a blanket over her chest as I lean forward to find the source of blood on her arm.

"Bullet's still in her shoulder, nearly through." My voice comes out void of emotion as I look up at our medic as he steps up beside me.

Quickly, he splashes the antiseptic over his hands before doing the same on her shoulder. Her body tenses but she doesn't make another sound. Axel grips the blade in his hand as I lean down and roll her towards me.

"Ember." Pain-filled eyes flick to me as I lean closer. "We have to get the bullet out."

She nods, not looking away from me. "It's ok. I know."

"Just hold on to me," I whisper, pulling her head into my

shoulder making sure to be careful of the cuts.

Her right hand latches on to my thermal to bury her nose in my neck as Axel brings the blade in. Her breath hitches, body going rigid in my hold. A gasp of air heats my ear as she lets out a whimper.

"Ty tak khorosho spravlyayesh'sya, detka. YA zdes,' lyubov.' YA zdes'." My words are a whisper into her ear for no one else but her as I hold her closer.

Viking grabs her legs as they kick out pinning them to the table so, Axel can make clean cuts. "I know it hurts, Emmie. Just hold on he'll have it out in a minute." His face is a mix of pain and concern as he watches his sister struggle in our hold.

The rest of our group watches with grim faces. She's alive and in our hands but the absences of Hunter doesn't bode well. Maskin and Mustang leave to keep watch more on guard now than before. We don't know if they are following her or if she got away without being followed.

"Got it," he says, pressing a pad of gauze to the fresh cut on her front and the entry wound on her other side. "I've got to stitch it up." His words a warning of more pain for her.

Viktor's large hands press over both sides of the wound allowing Axel to get the sutures ready. I try to focus on what needs to be done but the feel of her lip moving across my skin tests my resolve as tingles race down my body. Her strength in the face of what is being done fills me with pride because I know that she's hurting beyond measure right now.

I watch as the needle meets her skin for the first stitch. Throughout the entire thing, Ember does no more than moan and pant into my throat. God, I hate seeing her in pain. Stitching both front and back takes less than two minutes under Axel's capable hands.

After wrapping it up, he cleans the cut on her head and carefully stitches that as well. Thankfully, the cut on her throat and face are superficial, only needing to be cleaned. The ribs are only bruised not broken.

Chapter 18

The guys with Mikhail are fast and efficient as they take care of my wounds and work to warm me up. I'd thought I was out of my mind nearly on death's door when he caught me in the snow outside. I'm not sure how I got here but I need his sturdy presence to keep me grounded as they work.

When they finish, I refuse to let go of Mikhail, so he picks me up again and sits with me in front of the fire on the couch wrapping me tightly in blankets on his lap.

Someone hands him a towel and he quickly wraps my cold

hair up and off my shoulders. As soon as he finishes, I curl up closer to him seeking his warmth as the shivering takes hold. His big arms hold me close as the men gather around us.

I blink back tears as my brother sits on his heels in front of me. His hair isn't high and tight anymore but it's not long by any standards. His grey eyes burn with worry and determination behind a layer of whiskers that weren't there before as he studies me in Mikhail's arms.

"Emmie." His voice catches as he looks at me. He gently grips my knees.

"Where have you been?" I whisper angry at everything in the world right now. And because he's here now after everything it's all on him.

He shakes his head. "Emmie I."

"Don't call me that." I hiss making Mikhail tense around me. "You don't get to call me that after disappearing for all those years. Letting mom and dad think you dead."

He has the grace to look ashamed but still unmoved. "I'm not allowed to talk about that, Ember. I can't tell you how sorry I am, but right now, we need to know what happened. We found the shop trashed."

"Josey?" My heart leaps in my chest as I lunge forward as far as Mikhail's arms will allow in an attempt to get up to find my little girl. I didn't see her when the men pulled us from the car, and I hope she is safe. Fear grips my chest at the possibility that she isn't.

"She is safe with your parents." Mikhail's voice rumbles through me as he gently pulls me back rubbing my arms in hopes of calming me.

"Hunter hid her in a cupboard before they could find her." I can hear the pride in his voice at Hunter's quick thinking.

My breath rushes out in relief as I lean back into his chest. "Thank God."

A shiver runs over me as I remember that bastard telling me what he wanted to do to me. The images of what they could do to my little girl make me sick to my stomach.

"He was with them Mikhail," I whispered, grabbing his forearm hard enough to leave nail prints as my anger resurfaces anew.

Mikhail's hands still. Cupping the back of my head with a growl pushing me into his shoulder as bows his head. Deep breaths ruffle my hair as he works to calm himself.

Joe sits up straighter. "Who was with whom?"

"The bastard from the bar?" Mikhail vibrates with anger as he remembers our meeting leaning into me to press our checks together.

"Yeah." I push further into his chest as his heat starts warming my cold veins.

"Bar? What are you talking about? How do you two know each other?" Joe's voice has a hard edge to it.

I turn and stare down my brother as Mikhail grips my arms in warning. "None of your damn business is how," I say clearly so he understands my meaning. My husband is dead and the brother I remember only now reappears after pulling a disappearing act for six years. The man in front of me has no say in who I decide to spend my time with. I may have hidden myself for years after Jackson's death, but I will never be afraid to say that I was with the man now holding me.

Jumping to his feet Joe stalks away into the kitchen. He runs his hands through his hair repeatedly as he paces back and forth. He spins and punches the solid oak bathroom door before coming back to stand over us.

"You touched my sister," he growls, pointing angrily at Mikhail. When we don't answer to confirm or deny besides lifting my chin with a death glare, he loses it. "Give me one good fucking reason I don't gut you right here right fucking now you bastard!"

"Because you have no fucking say," I yell glaring up at him moving away from his reach before Mikhail can say anything.

"No say," he roars back at me. "You have no idea who he is!"

"Shut up! It doesn't matter how well you think I know someone. It's my choice who I want to spend time with or who I decide to fuck." I scream pushing myself to my feet as rage burns like fire in my blood.

"Knowing you didn't stop you from tearing my heart out, did it? I had watched my husband, the father of my children, be buried. Then I nearly lost Josey from all the stress of it. Then I wake up to you barely alive and suddenly disappearing from the hospital."

I have to stop for breath as years of hurt rush to the surface. My brother opens his mouth to respond but I don't let him.

"Hunter cried for you and Jack for months. Josey doesn't even know who the fuck you are! I listened to Mom cry herself to sleep for six months and watch Dad refuse to finish that stupid fucking truck hoping someday you'd walk through the door! Fuck you! You have no say in my life anymore! I'll do and fuck whoever the hell I want." I finish screaming as I turn heading for my bed clutching the blanket tighter.

"Ember!" Joe tries to follow reaching for me with disbelieving horror filling his eyes, but I rip the curtain across in his face cutting him off.

Ripping open the dresser, I pull out dry clothes to put on. I curse as the stitches pull in my shoulder and I struggle to pull the sweater on. I hear the door slam as Joe goes outside into the weather, but I'm too pissed off to care. I pull the quilts back and climb into bed. Making sure the thick fabric is over my head before I allow any tears to slip free.

I love my brother. We were like two peas in a pod all throughout all of our lives. He never pushed me away like his friends did to their siblings. I followed him everywhere as a kid and he always wanted me around. What he learned and did so did I.

The sight of him tonight for the first time in six years was something I had prayed for since he left. Never in our lives have I ever spoken to him like that. Not one single time. Tears fall faster as pain seeps into my system.

Chapter 19

Mikhail

While I knew that Ember and I's connection would come to light eventually, I hadn't predicted such a heated reaction. I had hoped we could discuss it between ourselves after dealing with this mess before moving forward because no matter which way we turned it was going to get messy. That was out now.

The whole team simply sat with their mouths open as she screamed at her brother. She ripped out my heart word by word and from the look on Viking's face as his heart was smashed to dust.

Being part of a group like ours means most of the men on their side had to cut all family ties. I knew it was never an easy decision. I felt sorry for them in a way, but they did it to protect them from what we hunted.

I see the tears in her eyes as she cuts her brother off from her with a snap of fabric. I also see the guilt and pain on his face before he goes out into the dark to fight his own demons. I feel my fellow leader's pain, but my heart pulls me to stay close to Ember. This is going to be a fucked-up situation no matter which way any of us turns. I'm just not sure how to fix it.

There is no way in hell she's going to fuck whomever she pleases either unless it's me. I'll leave a line of fresh graves behind if she even tries. Damn, this woman keeps tying me in knots. We haven't agreed on anything yet when it comes to us. Hell, I'm still arguing with myself that it's safer to just let her go.

"Let's head out," Axel says jerking his head for the rest of the group to go out the door. Before I can say anything, the door shuts with me still sitting where Ember left me.

Ilya's hand falls to my shoulder as he and Viktor stand up. "We'll be outside. You better check on your woman." His voice is low, so it doesn't carry far. I appreciate him having my back without question even though I still have no idea where I stand on the issue. I nod my thanks as they follow the rest of our team into the cold.

Getting up I walk toward the bed unsure of what to do. I stand staring at the faded pattern fabric listening to her quiet cries coming from the other side for several minutes before I can't take the sound anymore. Pushing the fabric to the side I move to sit on the bed at her hip. The mattress sinks letting our hips fall into each other as I lay my hand gently on her shoulder mindful of the wound.

"Malen'koye plamya," I start to say but stop as she lets the blanket slide down to reveal her tear-stained face. My heart drops in my chest, and I instinctually lay down and fit her against my chest.

"Everything will be alright," I whisper as she clings to me.

"I hate this," she whispers into my chest.

"Please don't cry."

"I'm sorry," she sobs clinging to me. I shush her as I rub her back. Holding her for long enough that her tears stop, and I think she has fallen asleep.

"What are you all even doing here?" Her voice sounds faint.

Sighing, I kiss her softly on her forehead before looking into her eyes. "Hunting the men who took you," I tell her honestly, because I refuse to lose the trust we've built together, and there is no hiding what we are here to do now.

"Good." She sinks limply against me as her eyes fight their way shut. "Stay. Don't let go."

"I'm right here, detka. I'm not going anywhere," I promise. Running my hand down her back, she slips to sleep safely in my arms. The past months of missing her next to me eases with her in my arms again allowing my body to relax around her. God, she does fit as perfectly to me as I remember.

I have no intention of falling asleep. The next thing I know, the light clang of a pot and pan has me shooting up in bed. The mattress beside me is empty but not cold. She hasn't been gone long but I'm still on edge with her out of my sight. Pulling the curtain aside, I see Ember reaching for something on the top shelf.

"Ember, it's only been a few hours. You should be resting." I stand, and move to wrap my arms around her to grab the jar she wants from a higher shelf.

"So?"

"You'll rip the stitches."

"I'm fine." She takes the jar but doesn't push me away, so I rest my head next to hers. Putting the container down she takes hold of the counter top edge. "How long have you worked together?"

"Ember."

"How long, Mikhail?"

Taking a breath, I rub my hands over her hips, knowing this was coming but wishing for more time. "Five years."

"You hunt for guys like the ones who have my son."

"Yes."

"What you told me before, that was all lies." Her voice only betrays her slightly as she turns to me. She does an excellent job of keeping the hurt from her face, but I can see the small lines of worry and anger she tries to hide. Fuck does she think I spent time with her only because I knew who her brother was?

"No." I shake my head and pull her chin up to look in her eyes. "They are my businesses. Just, not all that I do."

"The creep called you Bratva. You're mafia, aren't you?" She catches the hesitation in my body as she silently dares me to lie to her, so I don't. I'm not ready for her to know that about me, but I nod anyway. We need trust in each other to go forward.

"So how did you get tied up with my brother?" Her eye color shifts from blue to almost emerald as she holds my eyes.

"Our groups work together on issues the government can't openly sanction. We follow our own laws, but even we draw the line when it comes to certain things. Being bratva is not so different than what we are doing here. We employee people, make money and keep our city as clean as possible. Any type of trafficking we shut down by any means necessary."

I shake my head when she opens her mouth to ask more and let my hands settle on her hips. "I know that the way he left hurt you, but he did it to protect you from those we go after. There are things you can't know about what we do."

She turns to the wall but doesn't step out of my arms. One more small victory. Hurt and hesitation lace her voice as she finally gets out,"Are you going to do the same thing?"

Spinning her to face me, I grab both sides of her face, careful of her wounds so she can see how serious I am. "Do you still want what you asked of me before we fell? Is that still how you feel? It would be safer for you if we deal with these bastards, and I never come near you again. I won't deny that I want you by my side. That I can see a future for us together. I will also not deny that being with me has its own set of worries."

"I have kids." Tears gather in her eyes, and she turns to hide them. As if the presence of the children to care for would make her any less desirable to me.

"So?" What is she getting at?

"It's not just me. How can you be ready for that? Hell, I don't know if I'm ready for that in our lives. You could hate them, or they could hate you. If that happens, we will never be anything."

Chuckling, I smile wiping the tears as they fall down her cheeks, and step closer till there's no room between us. "An unbelievably amazing bonus. Finding Josey and holding her in my arms was like fitting a puzzle piece into place. She demanded that I bring you both back. They are a part of you. I don't want just pieces of you, Ember." I grip the back of her neck as she lets out a breathless laugh.

"She isn't afraid to speak her mind."

"No, she isn't. I want every last bit. You know that I have to do terrible things sometimes. That I have blood on my hands. I live my life outside of the law. Both sides of my life have danger, but I would never allow any of you to be hurt because of anything that I am or anything that I become involved in."

She nods up at me as more tears fall through a soft smile. "I know you wouldn't. Josey's the easy one to win over. Hunter is very protective of her."

"As well as he should be. That little girl is not as easy as you think. She demanded proof that I was telling the truth before she would agree to let me close. You've taught them well, Ember. I will always protect you and the children with everything in me. Do you want me to leave, Ember?"

I lean closer, almost scared to hear her answer but needing it. Her words will change more than just our two lives. They would force me into action to go against everything I thought I knew I wanted and needed before.

"You make me feel alive," she whispers rubbing over the stubble on my cheeks her eyes pleading the way they did in Harrisburg.

"Feelings mutual," I smile. Our admissions lighten my soul.

"I'm scared that I want you so much. I can't take another loss. But the thought of walking away hurts so much already. It hurt to leave that morning." Her lids close slightly as she whispers the words before gripping my shirt and tilting her head up to me.

"It was a shitty way to wake up," I chuckle, hoping to make her smile again.

"What if you find you don't want us anymore and you leave?" Her whisper drops lower as she shifts uncertainly in front of me.

"I will stand by my word till the day they put the both of us in the ground and on into the next life. I won't ever let you go if you choose to give us a chance. I thought I was doing the right thing by letting you go before but you have haunted me every day since. I know what I want Ember. It's you, your children and however more you will let me give us."

"You want me to have your babies?" Watery whimpers float into the air as I grin holding her closer so she can feel how much I still want her. She wraps her arms around my shoulders to pull herself closer.

"If I had my way I would lay you down and start right now. However, I am a greedy bastard and there are several men sleeping too close for my liking. It would be a pain in the ass to cover up so many dead men. We also have a child to bring home." Kissing her head, I groan as she shifts letting me take her weight.

"Kiss me…"

"Yes ma'am," I cut her off softly with a hungry claiming of her lips. Pulling her closer to cradle her to my chest like the treasure she is as I deepen the kiss. God, she's just as addictive as she was our first night. One taste of her and I'm lost.

"You fucking bastard!" Viking roars flying through the door.

I only have time to push Ember behind me before the first fist connects with my jaw. My head snaps back from the force as I let him land blow after blow until he takes us to the floor. This is what I expected to happen even if she told me to stay away. I allow him to work his anger out on me only blocking the blows to my face as Ember screams above us.

Chapter 20

"Joe stop!" I scream reaching to pull him off. I grab his arm as he pulls back to punch Mikhail in the face again. He twists growling like an animal as he throws me back into the table. My shoulder burns from the hit but I get back up and reach for him again as Mikhail grunts from a blow to the gut. "Stop! That's enough."

He tosses me away again sending me to the floor as he rains punches on the man under him. I try again but he hits me in the face as he pulls back again. I land awkwardly with a pained cry as both my face and shoulder burn hotter. He's so mad I can't get him to stop.

I pull myself up and see the skillet sitting on the still-cold burner. I pick it up unsure if I can actually use it on my brother. "Joe stop! Let him go!" I scream hoping he'll listen this time. Out of options I grip the pan in both hands and bring it down as hard as I can to the back of my brother's head with a scream.

The echo of metal striking flesh rings through the space as the rest of the team runs in the door with guns drawn while the ones who were asleep watch us with wide eyes from in front of the fire.

Everyone stops short, as I stand over my brother who groans gripping the back of his head as he lifts off of Mikhail. He stumbles up and to the side before landing beside the table allowing Mikhail to move.

"Ember, get back." Mikhail jumps to his feet and wraps me up swinging me behind him again as he watches my brother climb to his feet with the help of the table. His hand squeezes my hip as he widens his stance ready if Joe wants to come at him again. I grip the waist of his pants pressing myself closer to him.

"Fuck." Groaning Joe shakes his head before glancing over at me. "What the hell! You hit me in the head with a fucking pan Emmie!"

"You should have listened to me the first time," I say though it sickens me to hit him like that. "And don't call me that. Be glad it wasn't one of grandma's cast iron." He winces at the very real possibility it could of have been Gram's pans and not the cheap metal one.

"So…" Mustang trails off before rubbing his neck as he eyes each of us. "Should we get involved?"

"No!" Both men with me yell at the same time.

I step around and lift the pan with a hiss. "Wanna test me too." They trip over each other as they back out the door with their hands up in surrender and slam the heavy wood behind them. "Pussies." I snort leaning into Mikhail as he pulls me back to him.

"You are a dangerous woman." He laughs hugging me close.

"No shit." Joe rubs his neck with a grimace. "Did you have to hit me so darn hard Ember?"

"You owe me a new pan asshole." I pout looking at the bent metal in my hand with a disgruntled sigh.

"I need to eat something." I reach for another pan and set it on the stove to heat.

"Son of a bitch! Damn it Ember, sit the fuck down you're bleeding again." Joe shoves me back into Mikhail's waiting arms. "I'll make you something just wait okay." He reaches for the water and fills the pot.

I look down at my left shoulder to see a tinge of red. I guess my shoulder was burning for a reason. "Huh… I wonder why, Joseph Elijah." I can't keep the bite out of my voice.

His shoulders slump and he hangs his head for a moment. Turning around he grabs me abruptly. Locking his arms, he leans into my neck to whisper in my ear so no one else can hear. "I'm sorry Ember. I'm so fucking sorry for everything. I missed you all so much."

A small sob breaks free as I grab him in return and hang on. "I was so scared when you disappeared. I fucking needed you and you weren't there. I've missed my big brother so damn much."

"I messed everything up back then. It should have been me that day, not Jack. Not my brother. I just wanted to end everything. It took me a long time to figure all my shit out and by then I couldn't contact you. I'm so fucking sorry."

"Don't ever say that!" I hiss backing up to lock eyes with him. "Don't ever fucking say that again!"

"It's true sis." He brushes a hunk of hair out of my eyes.

"No, it's not. We still need you."

"You're stronger than you know sis." The pain in his voice equals my own as we stand there holding each other until someone knocks on the door.

"Is it safe yet?" Mustang asks with his head edging through the crack in the door.

"Get the fuck in here you idiots." Joe gripes, stepping back and turning to the stove. "Axel, check her shoulder."

Chapter 21

Everyone sits around the room eating the food they guilt Viking into cooking for them again when all he wants to do is feed Ember. She curls into my side on the couch an empty bowl on the floor in front of her. Her head lays on my shoulder staring at the flames with a troubled expression even as sleep pulls at her.

I pull the quilt higher over her. "Are you alright?" I ask rubbing her hip under the blanket.

"I will be when we've found Hunter." She looks into the flames as if they have all the answers.

Viking looks up from his chair frowning. "Tell us what happened."

"I took the kids to the shop to give Mom and Dad some time to themselves. It was getting dark when I heard the bell ring." She shakes her head. "I know that door was locked. I made sure of it before we did anything. I got up to tell them we were closed three guys were spread in front of me and a fourth was looking over the cases before putting a gun to my head." The whole team sits up at the words as Viking snarls.

She levels a look at her brother which shuts him up quickly. "I tried to get them talking hoping they would think I was the only one there but next thing I know Hunter's rushing out of the back room telling them to let me go." She shivers and I pull her close.

"They all looked at him and laughed. I pulled my knife, rolled to put myself between them, and told him to run. I cut the closet one and two others before four more came through the back room and sent me into one of the displays. One of them kicked the blade out of my hand before they all jumped on me. The rest is a blur as we all rolled in a pile of kicks and punches. Next thing I knew I was on the floor of a moving car and that bastard from the bar held a gun to Hunter laughing as he told me he was happy I was going to fight."

The need to move and tear something to pieces courses through me but I hold her harder. The only thing I can do to ground myself as well as to let her know I'm with her as her eyes grow distant.

Viking shoots out of the chair to stalk around the short distance that makes up the living room. Giving him a minute to calm down, no one says anything. We've seen what these bastards do to kids and now his nephew, my son is in their hands.

Fuck I really need to bloody something. Ember wants me and I refuse to let go. My woman. My children. The demons tear at my skin demanding what is mine to be returned. It takes effort to quiet them as I pull my woman closer.

Viking has every right to be concerned and angry. He sinks back into the chair with a sigh. "What happened next?"

"They were shit drivers sliding all over the road before growing a brain and looking for a place to hold up. Asshole put the gun on Hunter again and told me I was going to get them to the closet cabin. So, we started up Dillard's while loudmouth kept me entertained by what they were going to do to us. Not all of them made it." She smiles savagely at her brother's shocked face.

"Dillard's?"

"Yep."

"Christ Ember what were you thinking!?" He rubs a hand over his face when I send him a chill the fuck out glare having no clue why he's so upset but getting pissed that he is growling at my woman.

"That as long as I kept them in my woods they wouldn't be coming out. I admit I got ahead of myself and that's how I ended up here alone. If I would have kept my cool, I could have gotten Hunter out." She closes her eyes to hide her sudden tears of shame from us.

"Ok let's calm down for a minute." Mustang jumps in just as Viking opens his mouth again. "Tell us the rest."

"Like I said I got ahead of myself and took asshole for a ride."

"What'd you do to him?" Axel jumps in as Viking opens his

mouth again. He shoots the man a dirty look.

"I killed the bastard."

"How?" I'm slightly off put and turned on at the amount of venom in her voice.

"Let's just say his face isn't so pretty anymore." She grins at me and her brother as we glance at each other asking if she's capable of killing another human.

Fighter yes but I don't know if I even saw a killer hidden within her in our time together. When a mother is backed into a corner you never can predict what she will do for her young.

"Oh, come on I have to know how you did it now." Joker leans forward a bright gleam in his eyes as he starts rubbing his hands together in glee. Some days it's not hard to see how he got his call sign.

Viking and I send death glares which he ignores as Ember smiles an expression so deadly it makes me worried and turned on at the same time. I don't know what that says about me at this moment.

"We took a trip down the hill together. His face met the rock in my hand a few times. They would have had a deeper more meaningful understanding of each other, but some dipshit shot me before we could finish our conversation. It knocked me off balance and I ended up rolling the rest of the way down the slope and into the creek. Dragged myself out and headed up here to regroup."

She shrugs like it's no big deal as we all stare at her in shock just as Viking explodes.

"Ember-Lee Jessica Anderson Russell, I swear to God I don't know what's worse! It's a miracle you aren't dead from pulling such an idiotic stunt. In one of the worst areas in this county no less!"

"Wasn't my death I was worried about." Her shoulders tip up under my arm. "I've had wo…"

"Ember," I growl in warning slapping my hand over her mouth to stop her from saying anything more.

The image my brain conquers of what could and did happen to her is still fresh in my mind. She acts like the condition I found her in was just another day in her life and not the worst moment of mine. I don't think I'll ever get over seeing her in such a horrible state in the next ten lifetimes.

Viking works his jaw as the two stare each other down before he shakes his head and puts his game face back on. "Joker you're staying with Ember the rest of you get some sleep we leave in three hours."

"No way!" Ember jumps up out of my arm before I can stop her letting the covers fall to the floor. "I'm going with you."

"Like hell you are." Viking snarls standing to go toe to toe with her. "You're already injured. My team will find them and end this before anyone else gets hurt. This isn't up for discussion. You're staying right fucking here Ember." He levels a finger on her back in commander mode.

She crosses her arms and smiles making me jump to grab her expecting her to go after him with fists this time, but she surprises me. "Fine, I'll stay."

This isn't right. There is no way she's giving up this easily when it comes to getting her boy back no matter how much I want to believe it.

"Yes, you will stay here. You're already hurt," I say standing with Viking on this issue not trusting her tone in the slightest. The sight of her earlier in the night will haunt me to the end of time. The need to keep her safe adds weight to my words as I grip her tighter.

"Yeah, I'll stay right here alright. At least until you're gone and then I'll go get my son and kill the bastards with or without any of you." She shouts.

Spinning, she starts jabbing her finger into my gut with a deadly glare that has me backing up a step in surprise. "You can't keep me out of something I'm already in. Hell, I know this country better than anyone on this team. I also know where they're heading. You aren't leaving me behind Mikhail! That is my child out there and I will not be forced to stay here because you're afraid for me to get hurt again!"

Tears edge her eyes as she continues hitting me with every word that comes out of her pretty defiant little mouth. The pain, desperation, and determination shimmer just below the surface as she glares up at me. Can I truly hold her back in my own fear for her?

Anger fills me when I picture the boy out there by himself with those men. He'd already protected his sister without thought of himself, watched his mother fight for him, and get knocked out. Heard what they wanted to do to the both of them, had a gun held on him, watched his mother take one of them out, and saw her get shot before falling into freezing water. He probably thinks that she's dead or dying. Now she wanted to go after them and possibly put him through that again. How much more could the boy take? I'm about to snap at her when her brother beats me to it.

"That's beside the point!" Her brother growls leaning into her space. "I swear we'll bring him back Ember. We can't have you out there and do what has to be done when we'll you concerned about taking care of you on top of keeping Hunter safe!"

"I don't need you to take care of me! I've been trapping in these woods for years without anyone watching my back. I can take all of them out without being seen while everyone will be dependent on you to keep from getting lost or killed because that's what this country will do, and you know it."

"She does have a valid argument." Ilya surprises everyone by speaking in her favor. I whip around on him with a snarl, and he brings his hands up telling me to calm down. "Put your emotions aside and think about it."

"I hate to agree," Mustang speaks up next. "With her, we could split up without having to worry about one group getting lost or missing them because we are all in one group."

"This is nasty terrain, and we don't actually know if they made it to that cabin or not." Joker nods as do the rest of the team.

"You can't be serious." Viking shakes his head in disbelief. His need to protect her battles with having another asset to the mission.

I'm struggling with the same instincts myself. While we tend not to bring in outside help ourselves it's not uncommon to get local help when needed, especially in remote areas like this.

"You feel the same?" I turn to Viktor and Maskin who haven't said anything all night. The big brooding menaces could read a situation and act before most knew what was even happening thanks to their training in the Russian special forces. They also have the uncanny ability to pick the right people to take on missions. If they said to take her it would mean she was needed.

Both gazes lock on Ember closely for several minutes before nodding to me. Well, fuck me, because there really was no way I could get her to stay when the rest of the men said she was needed. I run my hands over my face in frustration. Could I chance her being out there?

Viking turns to brace his hands on the wooden mantel above the fireplace as he stares at her wedding photo. He pulls it down searching for answers in the other man's smiling face.

"I wouldn't stay behind even if he told me to," Ember says softly as she leans into her brother's side wrapping her arms around him. I force my jealousy away even though her arms don't belong around her brother. "Not for any reason. I am going out there to get my son." She looks over at me with a sad smile.

Can I stand her being out in the coming danger? Could I force her to stay without making her angry by tying her up till we got back? Did I want to face the consequences of what would happen if I did that to her? Fuck! I am under the boss of my brothers for a reason. I gave orders and expected to be listened to without explanation, but it isn't that simple when it comes to this woman.

Snorting he replaces the frame only to close his eyes. "None of us could ever tell you no least of all Jack." He pulls her close as he sighs heavily. "Let's get some sleep everyone we leave before dawn."

Shaking my head, glad that he made the decision instead of me for once. I stretch out with the rest of the team by the fire as everyone settles down wanting nothing more than to crawl back in that bed next to Ember. I don't need to push my luck tonight any more than I already have with a bad-tempered brother in the room with us.

"Go to the bed Ember," I say without opening my eyes when I feel her move closer. My body makes room for her of its own accord as she makes herself comfortable next to me with a snort.

"She isn't going to listen to a word we say at this point," Viking grumbles from on her other side. "Just let her be so we can all get some rest."

"Love you too." She singsongs to him setting the guys to snickering around us.

Viking lifts his head growling at everyone. They all quickly turn over and will themselves to sleep.

"Bitch." He hisses at her which just makes her laugh as I growl. Just because he's her brother doesn't mean he can talk to her like that. I'd reach over and beat him if she would let go of my arm. When she doesn't, I open my arm so she can lie down to curl into my side.

Making herself comfortable laying her head in the hollow of my shoulder before pulling the quilt over the both of us. Hand resting on my abs her leg slips over mine to settle just under the part of me wanting her attention even if it will get me killed.

Gritting my teeth, I catch her hand lacing our fingers together before they can wonder. I feel her pout as she squirms just to punish me for stopping her. This woman is going to be the death of me I swear. Hell, I might even enjoy the ride out as long as she was next to me smiling.

Chapter 22

I wouldn't have gotten anymore sleep if Mikhail and Joe hadn't sandwiched me between them. Their combined heat melts the rest of the ice from my veins, allowing me to relax and gain some much-needed strength. I'll never tell them just how bad I'm hurting.

By some internal clock, they both shift at the same time waking me up from a light sleep. A quick brush of lips to my forehead and a firm squeeze to my hip puts a smile on my face. Mikhail rolls to his feet and gives me a smile. Sitting up, I climb to my feet and stretch forgetting about my shoulder. Axel catches my grimace and points to the table sternly. I roll my eyes but do as he says. Man has a sharp eye.

After letting him redress the wound, I pull out my spare clothes and get dressed. Thankfully, I always leave a spare pair of boots here as well because my other ones are still soggy. The soft leather molds to my feet with the added benefit of the fur to insulate them from the cold. While they don't have the tread like my other ones these are perfect for the hunt we are about to head out on.

It takes some doing, along with some internal cursing but I managed to brush out the bird's nest that is my hair and work it into a side braid. I make sure to face the wall so none of them can see the pain on my face. My shoulder is sore as hell. Don't need any more of them on their case. No more ammo needed for them to try to leave me behind again.

My jacket was in the back room of the shop, so I head to the closet. Jackson's leather trapper hoodie still hangs on its peg; untouched for the past seven years. My throat becomes tight as I trail my fingers through the sleek cream fur. It's a shame that I've let it sit in the dark for so long.

Mikhail walks over and lays his hands on my shoulders His face is full of soft concern as he looks at me softly. "What's wrong?"

Mentally kicking myself in gear I pull the coat out, close the door, and sling it on. "Nothing."

Before he can contradict me, my brother walks back in and stumbles to a stop as he takes me in. His eyes lock on the coat, and he struggles to swallow. I watch him collect himself and start toward me. He locks eyes with me before pulling it tighter, taking the belt, and looping it around me. A million tales rush between us involving this piece of clothing. He smiles, giving me a quick hug then turns to lean by the door.

Shaking my head, I pull open the trunk at my feet that I use to keep my trapping equipment. I grab two small blades and shove them into each boot before I pull out an extra Bowie. I shove it under the belt at the base of my back pissed because I don't know what happened to my blade after losing it at the shop.

Next comes my great-great granddaddy's tomahawk which I settle on my left hip. I reach in one last time and pull out my loaded gun belt. As I buckle it on allowing it to lay over the blade at my back, I realize the group has gone quiet. Adjusting it so the colt's handle is just behind my hip I look up and frown at the men.

"What?" I demand as I grab the leather laces to brace it to my leg. Turning I pull my Henry repeater from the pegs on the support beam.

"Damn woman." Joker wolf whistles cracking a grin as he takes me in from top to bottom and back again. "Who are you, Francis Boone?"

Mikhail growls stepping in front of me, cracking his knuckles as my brother and I scoff together. "You mean Francis Marion dumb ass," Joe grunts from his spot on the wall.

Leaning the rifle against the wall I tuck two boxes of ammo in the large pockets of the coat. "Always figured myself closer to Mad Anne or Mary Donoho." Shrugging my shoulder, I grab a backpack and put in extra clothes for Hunter, a blanket, a canteen, and some jerky.

"Mad Anne?" Viktor shocks everyone by asking. Almost forgot the man was around he's so quiet.

"Revolutionary War scout and messenger. Did her best work with a rifle, hunting knife, and a tomahawk." I chuckle slipping the straps over my arms as I turn toward the group before shouldering my rifle. I grabbed my trapper hat from Joe and slipped it over my ears.

"Alright Axel, you're with Mikhail this go round." They all nod as I roll my eyes.

I swear he's more irritating now than he was before. Mikhail's arm settles on my shoulders, and I feel him chuckle as I jab him with my elbow when his lips brush the side of my head.

"You say you started up Dillard's, but which way did you plan on taking them?" Joe asks, his brow twitching as he glares at the two of us.

"Hadn't gotten to the turn off yet. Hunter heard me say the cabin and he knows it's too dangerous to go for the mine. We've all told him to stay away from that area. I was going to take them through the mine and lose them but like I said I got ahead of myself with the asshole." I shrug to roll the guilt of leaving my son away refusing to show it.

"Does he know the area well enough to stay on the right path?" Mustang cocks his head.

"Of course, he does he's in these woods with me ten months out of the year." I snort. "Everyone in this town makes a living outside one way or another. There are too many ways to get turned around and get killed if you don't pay attention."

"So, he should make his way to the cabin," Joe says.

I swallow locking eyes with my brother. "I hope he does. You said he hid Josey and then he saw me get shot. He's every bit his father's son. I can only hope he listened to our warning of how dangerous the mine is and stayed away from it. I don't know that I'd count on that from him though."

I can easily picture him trying to pull off what I was thinking about without me around. The image makes me queasy. While

I've been in the cave more than once, it isn't a place that I am comfortable with my son being in alone.

"Alright, so both teams head for the cabin. I've been gone for a while, so I'll take the trail. You head around the backside. Stay sharp and take care of yourselves. Follow Ember's lead the back country here is like nothing I've ever put you in before."

None of them scoff at his warning as they all meet eyes before nodding and that makes pride surge through me for my brother. He was always born to lead and to watch him lead these men puts a smile on my face.

"Don't fan out unless one of us tells you to. The roads are the easiest parts of this country. Do your best to walk in our exact steps. Hunter knows how to hunt and track but he also knows how to leave signs so be on the lookout for that because if he has any doubt about me coming for him, he knows my father and the town will. If you see him just sign what you want him to do, he'll understand what is going on." I meet everyone's eyes to make sure we're all on the same page.

"Good to know."

"If you thought my trail getting up here was bad you better tighten your boots and pull up your big boy pants now. The fun part is ahead of us." Several eye me warily as I grin at them before heading out the door.

Chapter 23

Ember and Viking weren't joking about the dangers of this area. We've rounded several rock outcrops and dropped into small tight hallows that are barely two foot wide. Most of the hills are not hills as an average person would think of them.

We simply can't go straight up because the incline is far too steep. The ground is littered with stones of all sizes and the snow-covered mud of the partial spring thaw doesn't make it any nicer to thread through.

If I wasn't aware of her injuries already, I would never know it as we follow her at a fast pace. She moves with purpose, never once doubting where she goes or where she sets her feet on the slick ground.

We thought that Viking moved like a ghost in this terrain but quickly realized that with his time away Ember clearly outmatched him. She is in her element and seems to never lose her breath or run out of stamina. We quickly adjust our strides so that our feet land in her tracks to avoid any of us slipping and sliding over gullies, hallows or down ridges after losing our footing several times.

As we round the bend coming through another hollow that had us nearly walking sideways, she stops so suddenly I nearly ran into her back. She holds her hand out to stop us as her head tilts as if she caught some out of place sound none of us have the ears to hear. Her hand reaches out towards us with the signal to get low and hold. The whisper of sound behind me let me know they followed her direction.

She motions me to wait and slips around the rocks before I can stop her. The line of curses running through my head as I grind my teeth waiting for her to reappear are things my mother would wash my mouth out and kill me for saying. I'm sure I never used half of them during my military career or even dealing with Bratva business.

My nerves stretch in agitation as the seconds slip into long minutes before she pops up a hundred yards ahead of our spot hunkering down to motion us ahead. I wave the team after me staying low as we follow her up and over another ridge.

She stays far enough ahead of me that I can't ask her what's wrong till she flattens herself on a large rock overhang and we spread out on either side of her. Before I can voice anything, she shakes her head and nods below.

"That's the cabin." She leans forward scanning the area. "There's no smoke, no tracks, and boards are still up. No one is in there." Her lip trembles with contained worry as her eyes dart around looking for any sign of someone being around.

I open my mouth to give her some reassurance when Viking's voice buzzes over the comms telling us his team is in position.

"We can't know that yet, Ember. We still have to look." I squeeze her fingers before I turn to acknowledge her brother.

"Copy, Viking, we're in position." The line is silent for a moment before he signals for both teams to move to the target. I meet her eyes giving her a firm nod. The flakes of gold in her eyes spark as she nods back before sitting up and jumping off the rock.

The six of us rushed to the edge, muttering curses in time to watch her slide down the slope and start walking toward the house without even trying to conceal her presence. Together we jump down after her slipping and sliding as we rush to catch up.

On the other side of the clearing, I see the rest of the team hurrying forward, weapons raised. Both groups round the cabin ready for trouble only to find Ember standing on the tree line staring out into the surrounding area fingers repeatedly clenching into fists as her body vibrates.

Angry about her reckless behavior, I storm up to her and slam her twitching body against my hard one. I drop my voice so that she is the only one who can hear what I have to say. "Don't ever do that again!"

Her eyes clear of worry to snap angrily at me. "You need to trust me when I tell you something. I told you no one was here."

"Nothing is ever guaranteed in these situations Ember you can't just run off. They could have left someone here as a sniper.

What do you think it would do to me and your brother if we had to watch something happen to you because you recklessly ran off ahead? What would happen to the children and your parents?"

I loom over her, bending her body over as I grit my teeth to hold my anger. "I know you want him back. We all do but you need to shut your emotions down before they get you or someone on our team killed." My voice comes out harsh as I glare down at her.

Her eyes flick to her brother's angry face before bringing them back to mine as her fingers press into my chest. Her whisper of acceptance is barely audible, but I accept it with a nod.

"Sokolov," Viking growls with a pointed look at both of us before focusing on me. His fingers flex like he wants to lay into me again for confronting Ember's actions, but he's as pissed as I am that she acted so rashly. He looks ready to say more but shakes his head to look at her in a stern stare for several seconds causing her to shift toward me even though her head remains proud.

"Good?"

Nodding, we share a look. Turning my attention back to my woman I wrap her braid in my hand tilting her head into my chest as I lean down to growl lowly in her ear. "Leave me like that again and I'll blister your ass so hard you won't sit for a week, and then I'm going to fuck you over a tree within hearing distance of your brother. I'll make you scream. Then I will happily take the beating your brother will no doubt inflict on me for touching you. I know how loud you get when I pound into that tight little pussy of yours, or maybe we can try a new hole. Do you understand, Ember?"

Her breath hitches, and her fingers hook in my belt pushing my thermals aside to teasingly graze over my skin as she pulls me closer. "I guess I'm lucky to know that you can follow through with all your extra promises."

She pulls away with a smile before I can respond, the fucking tease. Remembering our second night together, I can't wait to find her son and spend some time by ourselves. Gritting my teeth, I struggle to keep the smile off my face because she has had but a taste of what more I want to do to her. I've dreamed up millions of things to put her sinful little body through in the months since she left my room. Maybe I will end up tying her to the bed after all. The thought has some merit to it.

"Alright guys, looks like this is going to be even more interesting than we planned." Viking pinches the bridge of his nose as I stand behind Ember to lay my hand on her hip unable to stop touching her.

"We need to split up again but run parallel to each other. We'll run a hundred yards off the trail while you follow it. Hunter should be leaving sign so watch where you step, he'll make it as big as he can get away with but with the extra snow it'll be harder to see." Ember pushes the rifle up her shoulder waiting for everyone to agree with her plan.

I want to argue that we take the trail this time to give her a rest, but Viking locks eyes with me, both knowing she won't back down. Nodding his head, we each take a quick drink before settling off again. "Let's get moving."

Ember moves out slower this time. Her movements are no less sure but carried through with more caution as she sweeps the area for any sign of Hunter. I push back the burning desire to watch her every step along with the urge to lock her away back in the cabin till all of this is over.

I've worked with Viking for five years, and if she's anything like him, there will be no stopping her when she sets her mind. Until we find him, she won't stop, nor will she slow down. I won't slow down. No matter what it takes, I will bring that boy home to my woman.

Chapter 24

I feel Mikhail's eyes sweep over my body every few steps I take as we mirror Joe and his team as they make their way down the trail. I'm more careful here. I knew the cabin would be empty before we ever left but I had to hope that my gut was wrong for once. Gritting my teeth, I slow my steps the closer we get to the beginning of the entrance before sweeping out a few yards further.

I motion the guys behind me to fan out towards Joe as we take in the last two hundred yards. I circle out a bit wider as I near the rock face. Mikhail stays ten feet from me with each step of the way.

With no new sign under the lip, we make our way towards Joe who's waiting at the side of the tunnel. He nods to the ground at his feet. A small slide most would tell you is from a deer slipping spans a foot with a hard indent at the end that has dislodged the dead leaves making my heart pound. I kneel eyeing it for any other signs before standing. Mikhail lightly touches my hip for comfort as I nod to my brother. My boy took them to the mine.

This is where everything can go to hell in a handbasket if we don't all work as one. They are not going to like what I have to say. I forced the air out of my lungs softly as my shoulder set. "Leave two. One there and there." I point out where I want each person.

"Alexi," Mikhail gestures and the silent man disappears.

"Joker," Joe nods to the man who winks at me before disappearing. "Ember, you stay behind me and Mikhail the whole time."

"No."

"Ember you will do as you are told in this." Mikhail grips my arm with a growl.

My jaw ticks as I suppress an eye roll. "There's another entrance. I'll take my group and swing around to cut them off."

Joe rears back like I slapped him which has crossed my mind, the damn control freak. "Ember!" The asshole bares his teeth at me as his hand whips up to tighten around my arm. "Are you telling me you went into this mine by yourself? Cause I know my sister would have listened when Jackson, Dad, and I told her not to go in there alone."

"I wasn't alone." I just might have been the only adult but I'm not going to tell any of them that. I don't have a death wish.

142

They both groan as Joe steps back pinching his nose in frustration and Mikhail's grip tightens on my shoulder. "Jesus. Em, I know Dad didn't go down there with you." I cock a brow at him daring him to prove it. "Fine but you will listen to him and the team when they tell you something. Axel, you'll stay with us this time."

"Yes, Dad."

He growls throwing me a pointed look. He flings his arm out telling me to get moving. "Be safe."

We need to make time, so I set a quick pace as we make our way around the ridge toward the back entrance. I'd found it when I was hunting thinking it was just a cave. It shouldn't have surprised me that the tunnels of the mine branched out to other outlets.

This mine had three openings, but the third one opened to a five hundred straight drop to the river below. You'd have to repel down a hundred feet just to reach it. Even if the bastards we were after found it they wouldn't get away using that opening. We just had to control the back and the front.

An hour later we climb the rocks that lead to the entrance. I hunker down in the rocks leaving a clear view of it as we pause to catch our breath. I take a quick sip of water before handing it to Mikhail as I study the area we're heading into.

"This is it?" He breathes in my ear, and I nod. "We will have to crawl through that."

"Yeah, it will be a bit tight for you guys, but it opens up right away. We leave one on watch here they won't have trouble controlling the area with how narrow it is." A hundred yards of a narrow four-foot-wide channel stands between us and the hole. We'll have to climb down the eight-foot walls to get there. I looked up at him with a small smile when I read the look on his face. "Not happening."

Grunting in frustration he looks over at the guys. "Maskin."

The only one out of both groups I've never heard talk nods as he pulls the rifle from his back. His black hair curling along the bottom of his hat and tattoos just visible over the high collar of his clothes scream danger so much I want to laugh. Some wear deadly openly but more often than not it's the ones that look pure who are most dangerous.

I wait for him to look up and lock eyes with his dark ones. I'm putting all my trust in this team, and they can't let me down. He must read the silent message because he tips his chin to me before setting up his watch.

Before I can move forward, he lays his hand on my arm before handing me his night vision. Taking them, I nod in thanks as we turn to make our way down and gather in a line to head in.

"You stay behind me." My Russian growls shooting me a dark look trying to stare me down.

I nod without fighting because I know it won't get me anywhere. I've heard his tone countless times throughout my life, and it never pays to fight about it head-on. I'll follow his lead until I see that something needs to be done.

Sucking in a breath I push the sling over my head, so I don't have to hold my rifle as I pull my knife free. No way am I pulling my pistol down here. Mikhail slides in front of me before I can step into the darkness. I shake my head in annoyance as I step in behind him, leaving my hand on his back as Viktor lays his hand on my shoulder as he follows me in.

Mikhail slides his pair of night vision goggles on as he leads us deeper into the start of the maze of this mine. We slowly skirt around the many pitfalls and dead ends. It's not long before the faint smell of smoke hits my nose. I tap his right shoulder to direct him down the next turn. His arm swings back to tap mine before making our way further in.

It doesn't take us long to hear the soft murmur of voices talking and soon after we see the flicker of firelight. They made it a lot further in the tunnels than I would have thought. Letting my hand slide down to his belt I tug at it to get him to stop.

He doesn't question it as he halts and sinks down into a squat letting me slide up so I can press into his side to whisper into his ear. "Chamber on the right. Deep enough for shadows. Let me slip in and see if he's there."

"Together." His hiss is near silent even to my ear. "Or I will drag you back out and tie you next to Maskin."

Grinning, I press my lips to his jaw in a silent kiss. I wait as he tells the last three with us to hold. Slowly we make our way to the offset chamber and we each take a side so we can check both sides of the area to make sure it's clear to sneak in closer to hear what's going on. Calming my racing heart, we look at each other and nod before slowly making our way into the darkness

Three men sit around the fire against the back wall looking right into the flames, but I don't see my son. Unease rolls in my guts as I move closer to hear them muttering to each other. I cock my ear when I'm close enough but still can't make out what they are saying.

I feel Mikhail slide up beside me before his arm circles to wrap me closer to his side to keep me from moving closer. We sit in silence for nearly twenty minutes before he tugs on me, and I follow him back out of the alcove to rejoin the team.

We slowly head back the way we came for a good way before he stopped us, and we all huddled together to hear what he had to say. "Armenians." He hisses in distaste and the rest of the team stiffens around us.

"Hunter led them into the mine and got them turned around before getting away from them from what I heard. Four of them are out looking for him while the others wait."

"Shit! He could be back outside already." The unease rolls heavier in my guts than before.

"One of our teams will find him before he can get out." Mikhail sounds so sure of himself.

"They've been here all night and most of the day!" I hiss pissed at him for no reason other than my own worry. "They were already down here by the time I dragged myself back to the cabin and then like a fool I disregarded my gut and tried the cabin first giving him even more time to get out. Christ, I'm such an…"

"Do not finish that sentence!" Anger twists his words as he grabs and shakes me.

"I should have come straight here," I growl trying to pull myself away. Hating myself for putting my son in further harm. I should have listened to my gut, but I let my brother make the final say without any fight. God, I so fucking stupid!

My fingers ball into fists at the side of my head as I bend forward so the men can't see my almost uncontrollable rage. I bare my teeth at the ground. "I shouldn't have let anyone tell me otherwise."

"We all made a call and agreed on it. This is not on you. We didn't see any tracks before either group came in and both entrances are being watched he will not get out without being seen." Each word is accompanied by a slight squeeze as he tries to give me hope and calm. In my gut though I know my son will not be found in these tunnels.

"I have to find him Mikhail! I have to!" Tears pool in my eyes so I rip the goggles off to wipe angrily at them. They're stupid and useless in this situation. I need to pull myself together so I can focus and figure out where he went. But the thought of my son being out there somewhere alone and possibly hurt sends my heart racing in ever increasing dread.

"We will find him Ember." He cups my face so I can't look away from him. "I swear to you that everything is going to be all right."

Letting myself lean into his hands I take all the reassurance he's offering.

Chapter 25

The anger rolling off of my woman fills the space around us making us all edgy. Nothing I say seems to give her any sense of relief as she continues to berate herself silently. Helplessness burns through me hotter than when I held this strong woman down so we could cut a bullet out of her shoulder.

I've had to tell countless women that their husband or son wasn't coming home but I have never hurt as much as I do now. To sit here and watch the woman, I love, fall apart when there is nothing, I can offer but words.

All I can do is take as much blame as she will let me as I try to get her to stop thinking about all the dreadful things that could have happened to the boy already. I can imagine that more than good enough for both of us. Leaning forward, I keep her face still so our foreheads rest against one another, murmuring soft promises in her ears until she takes a shaky breath.

"Is there another way out?" Ilya's voice drifts over us as he shifts closer, laying a hand on her back to offer his own comfort. If I thought it was anything other than comfort out of respect for my claim on her, I would gut him right here and now. I push the unease away telling myself that it is my arms sheltering her.

I feel her body stiffen under my hands as she absorbs and contemplates his words. "Maybe." Her fists clench and lower to dig into the dirt at our feet. "There are enough tunnels that he could get around us without our notice but…" She shakes her head as a scowl pulls her lips as if she's fighting her instincts about Hunter's abilities again.

"Tell us," I urge gently.

"There's a chimney." I can feel her shudder under my grip and quickly pull her closer. "It'd be a tight fit for me with a pack, but I've done it before when I spooked a bear. You have to climb nearly straight up, but it leads out to a small rock outcrop ….. I'd say it opens up within a couple of hundred yards of Maskin." I tense but don't get to say anything as she continues. "He knows where it is it wouldn't be hard for him to step around the corner and jump up without them knowing even if they were right behind him."

Without another word, she jumps to her feet spinning to decide exactly where we are as she slips the goggles over her eyes again. Just as quickly as she started, she stops sucking in a deep breath as she steps back until she's pressed tightly against my side. Lifting my arm, I curl it around her shoulders as I wait for her to tell us which way to head.

Reaching, she slides her hand down to tangle her fingers with mine as she presses closer. "We need to move but we can't leave them here."

Nodding, I use our hands and push her forward. With a quick hand signal, I tell them to make it quick as I say. "Viktor. Ilya deal with those assholes then make your way out to Maskin. We're right behind you Ember."

Shoulders shaking in a silent fury, she steps ahead but pulls me up beside her. Without letting go of me she leans forward to study the ground relying on me to watch for any danger before we walk into it.

Humbled but filled with pride at the amount of trust she lays at my feet with each new unexpected turn we take in our journey, I grip her hand more securely as I let her move us along.

The darkness seems to go on forever as we make our way to the exit chimney hoping for even one small sign of the boy. Ember never takes her eyes off the dirt but seamlessly guides us around each turn with practiced ease.

I feel as if we have been traveling this way for hours when Ember straightens gripping my hand tight before hurrying forward until we come to a standstill in a cramped alcove that barely fits the two of us.

Before I can ask what's happening, she spins throwing her arms around my waist. "He went up." It's impossible to miss the slight catch in her voice.

"You're sure." I hate to doubt her, but we have to be certain.

"Yes. Look." I follow her fingers as she traces them down to some nearly indistinguishable marks on the wall. "Boot slide."

She explains without me having to say anything. Looking closer I can make out the top of the track as the rounded toe of a small boot. Too small for any of the men we were hunting but exactly right for a child. The child we need to find.

Hope, pride, and joy flare to life in my chest causing me to clutch her closer to me and drop a heated kiss on those soft lips that I can't get enough of. "You're incredible," I whisper in a voice dropping to a dark husky breath. Tucking some stray hair under her cap and behind her ears I lean forward to pepper kisses across her face. Her sweet breath fans over my face in a sigh as she curls against me.

Pulling myself back just enough to keep her in my arms, I drop one quick kiss before leaning back to look up at the shaft above us. My eyes narrow as I take in the close confines of the space. There's no way I'm going to be able to climb up with her, but I'm determined to try.

Stepping up to the rock I reach with both hands grabbing onto some of the rocks before setting my right foot against the stones. Heaving myself up. It doesn't take long for my shoulders to wedge against the stones around the small hole. Grunting I try to twist myself every way I can without any success.

Frustrated, I drop back down and pull her into me again. "I fucking hate sending you out there by yourself baby."

"Trust me. I know what I'm doing out here." She sighs cinching her arms around my waist. "These are my woods. I know how to get around unseen."

Cradling her face, I press a deep slow kiss on her plush mouth. "As soon as you get out you go to Maskin and take him with you, No one goes out alone. It is not safe. Do you understand me?"

Sighing, she leans into me as she nods into my chest. "I'll go get Maskin, before going after Hunter."

Her arms circle around my shoulders and her nose buries itself into the cool skin of my neck sending heat rocketing straight to my cock even if this is the worst time for those thoughts. God, I don't want to let her go out there by herself. I want to keep her next to me, in my arms, but we have to finish this mission.

"Good stay safe and don't get shot again. Both of you, watch each other's backs." Resting my check on the top of her head, I close my eyes for a brief moment.

"I'm scared," she bows her head to hide from me.

Shit, I internally curse. This is not the time for her to start doubting herself. "There is nothing for you to be scared of."

"What if I screw up again?"

Pushing her back, I cup her cheeks and pinch her chin so that I have her attention. "You won't. Follow your gut and everything will be just fine."

"I hate not knowing if I can trust myself."

"So, we deal with this shit and then never have to go through it again."

Her arms tug me closer as her fingers tunnel into my hair. The scratch of her nails is light but firm. "Who taught you to talk so sweet?"

Groaning, I rush down to claim her mouth in another kiss. Pushing her against the wall trying to devour her wanting every single piece of this woman. Taking her hips, I lift her to push between the warm set of her thighs swallowing the moan that pushes from her. Every small movement sends fire pulsing within my veins as I hold her tighter.

I want to own every part of her. I can't own her past but I damn sure will own and dominate every single second of her future. I bite back the words wanting to leap from my lips. They want to force their way out, so I deepen our kisses letting her feel all the need and want I have for her and her alone.

Jerking myself away I step back willing my body to still as our heavy panting fills the small space. Cupping my hands, I lean down. "Come woman up you get."

Her hands settle lightly on my shoulders before she lifts her foot into the well of my palms. As if we'd done it a thousand times before I lift us seamlessly for her to easily climb up the rock to miss the slick dirt that Hunter had to scramble up to get out the same way.

One foot on the rock, the other in my hands she grips the ledge ready to pull herself up but stops. Reaching down she grabs my jaw to press another kiss. "No matter how crazy and quick we've been…" My breath freezes in my lungs as I wait for her to finish. "Mikhail, …I… I love you."

Her confession lands like a hammer blow. All I can do is stand there for the space of five rapid fire heartbeats trying to calm my demons. Growling I lunge up and plunge back into her mouth. "You are mine. You, Josey, and Hunter. Mine now and forever."

"Mikhail."

"Hush." My finger seals her lips. "You asked me to stay. Told me not to leave. I fought myself every day since I first held you in my arms. I needed you safe more than I needed to breathe. Every moment away from you has been hell. "

"I'm stronger than you think." Her response is a breathy whisper.

"I know, moy malen'koye plamya. Josey is just as strong. I cannot wait to meet Hunter and be amazed at his strength too."

"You won't be saying that when they both decide to stand

against you." A soft smile plays across her lips.

"Josey already has my heart, as do you. Hunter and I will be fine. I'm never letting go of you and the kids. As soon as I get us home, I'm going to show you how much I love you. I'm going to fill you up until this belly is growing with our next child, who I pray looks just as beautiful as their mother." Taking her weight in one hand, I press the other against her womb as I make my promise. "Now get moving. Go get our son."

Chapter 26

The climb up the chimney is painfully slow. Each new handhold jabs dangerously into the palms of my gloves. My legs burn with each push as I step and lock my limbs with each breath. It's just as hard as I remember from the last time which I should find concerning considering the amount of damage on my person.

I'm grateful that it takes every bit of my concentration to navigate, so that I don't slip and fall back down the three-hundred-foot pitied shaft I've managed to climb so far. I need all my focus because I can't dwell on Mikhail's parting words.

As soon as Hunter is safe, we are going to have a long talk about what he said before sending me up this damn hole.

Finally, my hands grip the edge of the hole, and I pull myself out onto the freezing ground. Tossing my pack to the side, I roll onto my back. I lay there trying to catch my breath as I look up into the treetops.

My stitches burn and my shoulders feel like they are on fire. My limbs feel like jelly. I'm sure I opened my shoulder again in the climb. I'll give myself five minutes to stay here and catch my breath.

Alright time to move your ass, Ember Lee. Groaning I roll pulling myself together and snag my bag. My senses search the woods around me, but I don't see or feel anything out of place on this ridge line.

Before I head for Maskin, I look at the ground to find Hunter's tracks. It doesn't take me long to find which way he went. Relief ripples through as he follows the ridge in Maskin's direction more than half the way to the Russian's post. Quickly, I notch the tree where our paths will separate for a time with my hatchet and turn west to get my back up.

Pine and mountain laurel tangles work to slow me down as I make my way down the ridge. The many branches of the knotty brush are great for providing me with ample cover, but they also make it so that I need to move so much more carefully to avoid tripping and hurting myself. Forcing my body to forget about the pain of my injuries as with each step, I focus on slowing my breathing. I'm getting closer to the entrance.

Ten more minutes of navigating the laurel, I stop a hundred feet above the opening still well within the covering of the dense branches. It's a blessing that the storm has passed, and the sun is shining, but not for long as shadows already stretch around me. A quick glance up tells me that it's around four already.

Those bastards grabbed us nearly twenty hours ago and I don't know how long Hunter has been out on his own. I need to move fast but Dad didn't raise a complete idiot. Instead of rushing into the open and risking getting my head blown off, I have got to move smartly.

Pulling my knife, I crawl forward purposely giving the branch on my left a light shake to make the leaves dance for just a breath. Once I know I have enough light I tilt the knife so that the sun flashes across the blade to get Maskin's attention before using the same light to tell him to meet me over here.

I'm close enough to the edge of the tree line so that he can spot me without putting myself in the open enough for a kill shot. Pausing for a beat I send the same signal another two times before I lay back to wait for him.

A few moments later, I hear the soft rustle of a body moving through the thicket in my direction. Sitting up, I grip my blade as I settle back into the shadows just in case it isn't who I think it is. I watch as the noise moves closer before I see him make his way through the tangles to my side.

Kneeling beside me, he scans the woods before giving me his attention without taking his eyes off our surroundings. "Where are the others?" His accent is much heavier than Mikhail's, and it takes me a moment to get through it to his words.

"Hunter got them turned around in the caves before, losing them and climbing out the shaft I came up. Mikhail and the guys couldn't fit. Too tight for them. They are dealing with part of the group we found, and I promised to get you before going after Hunter. He followed this ridge before turning north Fifteen minutes back." I jerk my head in the direction I came.

"Let's go." He grips his weapon motioning for me to take the lead.

"Watch your footing; we'll be out of this mess in twenty minutes than we can make up time."

Together we work our way back up the ridge of strangled laurel branches, twisted hemlock, and large loose rocks. For such a big man, he follows me with little sound to no and no complaints about the terrain.

In the thickets, our pace is slowed but as soon as we leave the thickness behind, we move out faster. Our determination to find my son has us moving at a much faster pace than when we were in the larger group.

We make it to the base of the ridge in good time. I want to keep going but I force myself to stop and drink a few sips of water as well as eat a piece of jerky. Most of the day is over, and I've barely eaten anything since we left the cabin before the first light. My stomach wants to rebel as soon as the first bite hits it, but I choke it down and finish the small chip of venison. Maskin sits beside me taking small sips out of a flask.

Without a word spoken between us, we get up and begin making our way up the next mostly gentle slope. Nothing is gentle about the area we're in. There is no more snow. The storm finished blowing over while we were in the mine. The temperature has dropped at least ten degrees allowing the wet to start firming under our feet. A blessing and a curse, it makes the tracking easier but the icy footing more treacherous.

The tracks are light and far apart. Scuffs on rock edges are part of the barely noticeable signs of his passing that I can see. Near the bottom of the decline, he lost his footing, leaving a full-body slide before he could regain control. I won't let myself feel worry just as Mikhail told me, we will find him.

A small creek taunts me twenty feet ahead of us as we continue forward. Here the tracks vanish. The opposite bank is clean of any prints. The water seems to be only one maybe two feet deep but if the current is strong enough it could have washed his feet out from under him. Did he go across as his tracks suggest or did he back track? Shit, what do I do? Mikhail's words flash through my mind and I stand up straighter.

"Wait here." I wave for Maskin to stay back as I step down from the rocks into the water. Taking my time, I make sure each foot is solid before moving on. The water here is beyond freezing. Coming down from small natural underground springs they never stop running due to the heat or cold. It doesn't take more than five steps before the water is rushing against my knees. I shift my feet further apart to keep my balance as I stand checking the banks around me.

There's no sign of him as far as I can see in either direction. Closing my eyes, I gulp in a deep breath. He knows this area. He knows how to survive. Which way did he go? Downstream would take him further into the logging roads making him easier to follow. Upstream would make it harder to track over the rocks but lead him closer to our cabin.

"Here." Maskin's voice pulls me back around.

Making my way to the bank thirty feet from where he went in is a tiny scuff mark so small only a trained tracker looking for it would notice. My eyes narrow in focus as I study the mark. Pride fills my soul as I follow the traces of movement to the small perfect hand print as he makes his way upstream.

"That's my boy." I grin as Maskin reaches down, pulling me out of the water and onto dry land.

The sun is fading fast but the clues he leaves behind allow us to chase faster than most would consider safe. Maskin, bless his soul, keeps pace without uttering a word of complaint. Both my brother and Mikhail would nag me to death about not being careful enough. My brother should know better, but Mikhail has plenty of time to figure it out. The thought brings a smile to my lips. He's going to have a lot of things to get used to if he genuinely wants us.

My eyes stay trained on the trail in front of us. I rely on Maskin to watch our surroundings. I have always worked alone but he makes it natural and easy to be a team.

As I round a section of jutting rocks, a heavy figure slams me off my feet. My back slams into the rocks I just came around as a shot rings through the air. Pain burns along my ribs from the impact. Only muscle memory saves me from the blow aimed for my heart. There is no room to fight here I have to move.

Jumping to the right I let myself roll. Spinning mid-roll, I catch a glimpse of Maskin fighting another man, so this one is on me. He's moving too fast and close for me to pull either of my guns. The heavy handle of my knife settles into my right hand as my left rips the tomahawk from my belt. My first swing takes him by surprise and his gun disappears in over the edge.

Chapter 27

By the time I make it back to the rest of my team, the group of filth has already been dealt with and they are going through things to give us leads on how to shut down the group. Their grim faces tell me they haven't found much. It's the same with every small group we manage to eliminate.

"Your woman was right, boss. These men are truly idiots," Ilya states coming to stand next to me. "No proper clothes or equipment for anything but grabbing who they were after and running back to their dark little nest. Only had guns, a few needles, and the clothes on their backs."

Shaking my head at the ill prepared thrash, I wait as Viktor joins us before speaking. "Hunter made it out through the hole Ember told us about. She followed him up, but I couldn't fit, so she's going to pick up Maskin."

"Not to step on toes, my friend, but is it truly safe to send her out on her own? We don't know where the rest of the rats are running around. They could still be down here, or they could have found their way out." Ilya shifts kicking the body of one of the dead men at our feet.

"No, nothing about any of this is safe for anyone. I like sending her out there even less than you, but there wasn't much of a choice," I agree worry clenching my guts into knots before I push it all out of my head again. "However, she isn't alone. Maskin will not let anything happen to either of them without a fight to the death."

"Then let's get moving." We retrace our steps, moving faster to get us out and regroup with the rest of the team.

A sound behind us has us dropping to the floor and pulling our weapons free. We hold our position. Each man is several feet apart so our numbers are hidden from view. The faint shuffling moves closer until each step is identifiable in the still air. Counting each footfall, we wait for the three to make their way around the corner.

As soon as the last one steps into view, weapons are raised and orders are shouted. The recognition of the voices has us all breathing a sigh of relief as safeties are clicked on and barrels lowered. Viking and I step forward to roughly slap each other on the back as our group comes together again.

"Well, that's one hell of a way to wake up." The big man shakes his head with a grin.

"Better than a bullet I suppose. What did you find?"

"Your gifts a mile back, but that's it."

"Those three got separated when Hunter gave them the slip. Not sure where the others are. Just know that they are still looking for him. Ember and I found where he got out and she went up the chimney after the boy. We couldn't fit to follow her up. She promised to return to Maskin before going any farther."

"If she said she was going to, then she's got him with her." Taking a breath, he nods his head in assurance. "Let's get the hell out of this hole and find them."

Coming out into the faint light of the sinking sun lifts a large weight that I wasn't aware of from my chest. With each exhale my worry lessens.

Quickly climbing up the rocks, it's a relief to see that Maskin is nowhere to be seen. Each of us scans to surrounding ground till Viktor's quiet call brings us around to the spot where Ember and Maskin rejoined. With a quick comms, Joker and Alexie are on the move to intercept us.

"They left a trail any of us can follow." Mustang cracks a grin being that he is the worst tracker in our group. The storm has blown itself out for now leaving a clear unbroken path before us.

We all share a quick laugh, letting Viking take the lead so we can get the hell out of the endless tangle of vegetation that seems to go on forever. It doesn't take us long though and we are on the other side moving faster than before. Not long after our last two slip seamlessly into formation before the trail veers off the easy way back to the abandoned cabin and farther into the woods.

At the edge of a stream, we all pause while Viking steps into the current to see which direction they are headed when the trail doesn't reappear on the other bank within eyesight. After a few moments of walking downstream, he turns around and heads upstream looking for where they came out. We stay where we are not wanting to muddy the trail.

At his whistle, we make our way upstream as he comes out of the water on our side of the bank. "Heading further into the mountains."

"Why would he run farther from help?" Axel scratches his head in wonder. "Is he turned around?"

"He's not." Viking grins. "He's a little asshole just like his mother."

"Viking." Words of denial are on the tip of my tongue, but I hold them back as he starts laughing.

"Calm down, man." Viking still cackles. "Upstream is deeper into the mountains and a hell of a lot harder to navigate but I'll bet you a month of pay that kid is making his way back to the trapping cabin. He covered his tracks so they couldn't find him, but Ember and Maskin are making a highway straight to him."

"Why wouldn't she cover her tracks?" Mustang asks.

"Because she wants them to come after her. She's covering Hunter's tracks with her own and leaving signs to show that she's not dead." He points to the fresh slash marks on one of the close pine trees. "Once she has him beside her, I'm sure she'll try to give Maskin the slip to turn around and hunt the bastards by herself until we catch up."

"Stop talking and let's move." My words are a low growl taking them by surprise as I push past knocking shoulders as I go.

I can picture my woman trying just that far too easily. The woman is hurt and should be sidelined but she's out here. She's out here hurt and out hunting our elite team. Of course, she would try to slip Maskin and go for blood by herself. We must catch up before that happens.

She may not be hiding her trail, but that doesn't make her any easier to follow at all. I thought that the rocks we went through before we rough but the minefield of them that we have to move through are on a whole different level of difficulty.

Even watching my footing, I've rolled my ankles over two dozen times on hidden gravel patches. Joker completely lost his legs and side ten feet before gaining control again. Even Viktor and Ilya are grumbling under their breath as the terrain seems to get worse instead of better the farther, we go.

At the edge of another dense patch of pine, we stop to catch our breath and take in some water when a bird call has Viking going still.

He holds up his hand before anyone can say a word. His head tilts as the notes continue for another minute before going quiet. His lips press as if he's about to whistle back when another bird call filters through the air. The first bird answers back with a slightly different cadence and the other answers back.

"Ember found Hunter." Viking's voice betrays his relief. With a breath, he sends his own bird call into the air to which the first bird sends another cadence back.

"Dude, that was just birds." Mustang shakes his head. "We've heard those calls all day."

"I know that you're the newest to this team, but you were required to read the same things as the rest of us." Ilya sighs looking at the darkening sky.

"Seems like we're going to have some review training on old-time tracking and hunting when we get home." Viking gives everyone an annoyed look. "Ember was the eastern towhee, and Hunter was the cardinal that answered her."

"They're just ahead of us." I cut them off as I step forward again with Viking at my side. *We're nearly there baby just wait for us a little longer.*

A few hundred yards down just before the next rock opening, we come to a quick stop as a body lays haphazardly off a low rock face. Laurel bushes conceal most of the body. Blood drips from the served windpipe and several stab wounds. Large wide gashes line the body's rib cage. There are marks on his arms and legs as well.

"This isn't Maskin's work." Viking and I lock eyes as we digest the savage work that ended this man's life.

Chapter 28

The path is clear enough for me to see that we are only moments behind him. I check myself at the edge of the small clearing. Rushing in will only make him hide if he hasn't heard us behind him. My silent shadow pauses at my side sweeping the same area as I am. Nothing moves and the birds are singing their normal patterns. Still doesn't hurt to see if he'll answer my call. Pursing my lips I use the northern towhee call.

Props to the man for not looking at me like I grew another head as we wait for a return. After a moment I try again and then a third time. My heart squeezes in fear as the silence around us continues. Did something happen to him?

Before I can work myself the notes of the cardinal sound off in the correct cadence. Hunter's dark head slides around the edge of a pile of thick twisted laurel as I slide down the rocks leaving Maskin farther behind in my hurry to reach him. His big hazel eyes find mine as they swim in relief when he sees me.

"Mom!" Crawling out of his hiding spot he runs into my arms.

"Oh, thank you, God." Tears threaten to break past my defenses. "Are you hurt anywhere?" Pushing him back I sweep my hands over his shaking figure before pulling him close again when I don't find anything.

"I'm ok."

Just as I'm about to take my bag off to get the blanket his gasp of fear has me spinning around. Maskin is slowly making his way down the last few feet. At my sudden turn, he whips around to scan the trees behind him. When neither of us senses anything I give him a shrug and a small smile.

With a smile on my face, I kneel down to bring Hunter's attention back to me. "He's a friend, ok?"

The big man comes to a stop a few feet from us while Hunter pulls his shoulders back. Tipping his head, he looks the big Russian up and down for a solid minute before looking back at me. At my nod, he steps up and offers his hand the same way he's seen my father do countless times.

The first emotion I've ever seen crosses the big man's face as he kneels down to my son's level and takes his hand in his own. His voice is just as raspy and thick as before. "Well meet little one. Maskin Ogarkov at your service."

Amusement creases the edge of his eyes as Hunter grips his

hand with a firm nod before answering just as formally "Hunter Russell sir."

"How about we get somewhere we can spend the night?" I drag their attention back to me in the last of the light.

I twist my head thinking about the closest safe space for us till the other catches up. Joe isn't far behind us from the volume of his call just minutes ago. I won't be able to slip away to hunt like I planned to now that my son is safe but that's just fine. There will be time enough for that fun tomorrow.

"Just up this ridge is a shallow cave we can use while your uncle and the others take their sweet time. You'll be fed and warmed up before they find us." The normally silent man runs a hand over his mouth to hide his grunt of amusement but both Hunter and catch it.

After a bit of a climb, that leaves me more winded than I will ever let any of them know we make it to the place I want. I wave Hunter back as I make my way in to search for any occupying guest in the space that we need.

There's a narrow five-foot entryway before it makes a sharp turn that opens up to a room roughly ten by eight. No smell or tracks catch my senses as of yet. That's good. Finding nothing I step back out and wave the two of them into the darkness.

As the two of them look around the space using Maskin's flashlight while I go to the back wall and pull a handful of dried grass and twigs into a nest. One stroke of my knife over the ferro rod lands sparks on the fibers. Several well-timed puffs have flames licking the kindling allowing me to add some bigger pieces.

Maskin shoots me a look that has me grinning in fake innocence. "Yes?"

He rolls his eyes but doesn't say anything. Maybe he's trying to figure me out. Maybe he doesn't like me yet. I might actually be sad if that's true. I like the big silent man.

My pack slides down my shoulders to land beside my son. Ruffling Hunter's hair to hide the grimace of pain from the hole in my skin that I'm sure broke open at some point today.

"There's dry clothes and a blanket in there for you. You get changed while I go cover our trail up here alright?"

"Are they still after us?" His big eyes blink up at me.

"I'm not gonna lie baby. Three of them aren't going to be a problem anymore. There could be more of them, but your uncle and the others are still out there, so I don't know how many are left. I promise they won't touch you again."

"Uncle?"

"Yeah, Uncle Joe is on his way."

"Really! He finally back?" He leans forward and hugs me. "I knew he would come back to us."

"Yeah, he always comes back when we need him." Patting his hair before pushing him back to look him in the eye so I can brooch a more serious subject.

"Things are gonna change Hunter I promise. There's someone just as determined to keep us as safe as your uncle. Someone I believe we need in our life. What do you think about that?"

"A guy?"

The silent man breaks his silence for the second time as he chuckles from his spot. I will find the man under that mask someday. I smile at Hunter with a nod.

"So, is he gonna try to take Dad's place?"

"No Hunter he'll never replace your dad. No one ever could but I think we have enough room in our lives to include him."

His little lip pouts as he thinks about it. "I'll give him a chance for you mom, but he better watch himself."

"Thank you, stay here I'll be right back."

"Yeah. Love you, Mom."

"Love you more." I ruffle his hair as I get up.

Maskin follows me out but stays at the entrance as I make my way back down to make a false trail. His rifle is cradled in his arms as he watches the surrounding shadows with keen eyes. Making sure to walk as sloppy as possible as I go around the cutoff and then step backward so it seems like more than one person making their way through the snow.

Ten minutes later I cover the last few feet to the cave while covering our back trail to where he still stands guard. His eyes sweep over my work with a critical eye. When he looks at me again, I get a nod of respect before he motions for me to step back into the shelter of darkness. As soon as I step back into the room Hunter jumps up to hug me. I kiss his head and reach for the pack lying on the floor.

"Here you both need to eat." I pull the bundle of jerky from the front pocket and give our guard a pointed look. "Eat Maskin you haven't all day. Water and your flask don't count."

The big guy's jaw works for a minute as he watches me ready to argue.

"I can take watch while you eat."

"I can go much longer without eating. You two rest. I will stay on watch."

"Sit." I say sternly, pointing to the spot next to the fire. "Five minutes won't kill you."

Apparently, mom voice works on big scary Russians, because the man sits down with a grumble. Hunter shoves a piece of meat into his mouth to cover his giggles when I put the big man in his place.

He turns to lift a brow at Hunter when his laughter can't

be muffled. "Do you have something to say?" he asks with a straight face.

"No sir." My boy shakes his head.

Smiling, I kiss the top of his head as I make my way to the opening.

I don't make it more than a few steps before a grip on my wrist pulls me back. "Take this."

"I have a rifle." I say eyeing up the gleaming barrel of his rifle.

"Take it." He shoves it at me forcing me to take it or let it drop.

My eyes are big as I stare down at the smooth metal in my hands. The well-worn wooden stock feels light in my hands as I run a thumb down the barrel and over the suppressor. Wood adds weight, which is why most use carbon fiber stocks, but I would trust this gun over any new models. Not many snipers use wood stocks anymore but when you find your fit you stick with it. Warmth fills my eyes when I look up at the man. Snipers don't let anyone else touch their rifles, so I know this is a huge show of respect. My fingers tighten as I give him a nod.

Back in the gathering darkness, I sit within the shadows of the rocks. Hidden from view I can see a large area in safety. Nothing is moving as I lean back into the dark. The next few minutes go by in the same manner before the crack of a twig breaks the silence. Snapping my eyes in the direction of the disturbance, my fingers tighten on the gun.

On the lower ridge across from me, one of the men who took us stands silhouetted in the last of the day's light. The anger that simmered in my veins all day suddenly boils as I watch him walk ten feet to the left before walking back to the edge of the drop off.

Crawling forward on my stomach I lift the scope to my waiting eye. His familiar smug face fills the sights pulled tight in angry frustration. Vin's little buddy who wanted to join in on all the nasty shit he wanted to do to me stands in the cross hairs of my scope. His hand drags and pulls at his messy hair as he stomps around. Shifting the gun to scan the area around him but I don't see anyone else. Unease bubbles in my gut becoming worse with each passing second. Something is about to go down.

The gun returns to focus on the man as I feel Maskin's presence settle down at my side. Ignoring him I watch as he throws his head back in anger. Angrily he stomps back and forth. Each pass seems to make him more unhinged. The safety clicks off.

His focus snaps to the path below him and he pulls his pistol from beneath his coat. A quick shift of the scope brings Mikhail, Joe, and the rest of the group making their way between the rocks. The rifle snaps back to the man as I bolt a round into the chamber. This fucker is not touching my guys. Not one of them. They are all mine. My family and no one is going to lay a finger on any of them while I'm around to put a stop to it.

His big hand lands on my shoulder in a firm grip just a moment after I feel him bring my rifle around to get a look at what I have. "He is alone. You have this." Those rumbling words calm the butterflies working on getting out.

His unwarranted faith in my ability has my spine straightening. A deadly calm presence settles over me. Everything that my father taught me surges to the front of my mind and my body simply flows with the needed actions. No thoughts are needed, my muscles remember what needs to be done.

"One breath in."

"One breath out." He finishes softly.

With a gentle caress, the trigger responses to my finger as it follows my breath while on the other end of my sight, the man's head jerks back misting the snow behind him in red. His arm lowers slowly. Unresponsive fingers uncurl and drop the pistol to the ground at his feet. Blank eyes stare up at the sky as his limp body slides down off the rock face to the ground right at our teams feet.

Not today motherfucker. Not today.

Chapter 29

Mikhail

Rifles snap to readiness as everyone drops to find the source of the shot without worrying about the body at our feet. If we hadn't been listening so closely we would have missed the soft discharge of a silenced high powered gun. Even with our guard up we barely get a breath in before the man landed. Scanning the rocks and trees surrounding us reveals nothing. Nothing but the wind shaking the pines. The hairs on the back of my neck are standing on end as a lone bird calls out from the dark woods. Not a sound stirs the still air for several moments leaving us all on edge.

Before any of us can speak another bird call has Viking relaxing. It takes a minute for my mind to catch up to which call was sounded but as soon as I remember I'm hurrying across the ground towards the source. We are caught up with at least Ember and Maskin. I can only pray that Hunter is tucked in with them. The men aren't far behind me eager to have the group together again.

Eyeing the area for signs of passage I slow down considerably in the last of the dying light, but their trail is completely gone. The ground is completely bare. Not a trace of anything passing through. Where the hell did, they go? I need to get to my woman and my son. There's a sense of urgency to get them close and keep them there. I need to hold Ember in my arms; and lay my eyes on our son. I need to see them and know that they are indeed safe.

Ember's soft signal floats into the air stopping me from dropping down into the next hollow. Straining to see in the faded light I come up with nothing again. "Ember?"

"Zdes'" Maskin calls coming into focus twenty yards up the slope on my left.

My feet fly up the slope without regard for my own safety and I thankfully make it up without injuring myself. They're here. Just feet from me. Soon to be in my arms safe where no one can ever hurt them. I push myself faster until they stand before me.

Slinging my rifle over my shoulder I don't slow down as I lift my woman into my aching arms. Up she goes as we continue forward, legs hitch up to wrap around my waist to hold us together. Leather-encased arms cinch around my shoulders as her fingers plunge into my hair for leverage. Neither of us utters a sound as we steal each other's air in desperate pulls.

I'm not a crying man but I could weep at the feel of her in my arms again. To see that she is safe and whole. To be able to breathe again without my chest aching. Gently setting her feet on the ground we break apart but keep close. Leaning my forehead against her hair to breathe in her sweet scent I work to calm down. "Are you alright? Hunter?"

"We're all fine. Hunter's fed and sitting in front of the fire."

Giving her one more kiss I pull back with a smile and a lightened heart. Turning to my friend. "Good shot my friend."

"Not me." His dark eyes flick to the woman still curled up in my arms. That's when I notice the rifle in his arms. The brown stock is familiar but that is not his. There is no bolt action but a lever. Why does he have her rifle?

"Ember?" My brow raises at the woman in question.

"Yeah, Ember." The back of her hand bounces off my chest. "Only men can shoot now? Can women do anything by themselves or must we wait for the stronger sex to do everything?"

"Hush woman you're more than capable, and you know that. Now let me go meet our son." I have to laugh at her attitude.

I rock back slightly on my heels as she slams into me with a quick kiss which is over far too quickly for my liking. Eager hands snap around her arms before she can run off and pull her back for my lips to plunder more thoroughly. Fuck her brother and the rest of the team making their way up behind us.

"Come on." Threading our fingers together she pulls me into the dark impatiently. I have no time to reach for my light before she turns us, and we step into the small cave. A small fire crackles against the back wall lighting up the space well enough to make out the small figure that jumps up as soon as we enter.

Without thought my feet stop moving as my eyes hungrily run over the boy's form. My breath nearly cokes me as my throat tightens, stalling my air as I take him in. Eyes just as intense as my woman's are the only thing of hers that he took from her looks. Every other aspect of the boy is an exact replica of his father.

Letting go of Ember's hand, I slowly make my way to the boy and sink to my knees so I can look him in the eyes. It takes restrain to not simply fall before him and scoop him into my arms. He has a few scrapes and a little bruising on his face, but he stands before me safe and whole. My shoulders nearly sag as the fear of him being harmed lifts.

"You have your mother's eyes." My voice sounds strained even to myself, and I take a second to gather my emotions.

He darts a look over my shoulder before bringing those eyes back to me. He may be unsure but I admire that he is standing firm. "You're the guy mom told me about."

"What did she tell you?" I hold my breath waiting for his answer. Ember said that he would be the one hardest to win over. I need to know where my son stands so that I can make sure this works for all of us because I will not be letting my family go. Her brother will just have to live with it.

"That you were gonna protect us. That we should make room for you because she wants you around."

"Do you think that me being around is a good idea?"

"I don't know." His face scrunches up as he thinks. "I want Mom to be happy. She's been sad for a long time since Dad died."

"I want her to be happy too."

"You aren't my dad though." His little eyes harden as he delivers those words. His arms are crossed. and he gets the same look I've seen on his uncle more times than I can count.

Fighting back the smile that wants to erupt I respond as seriously as him. "No one can replace your father. Hunter, but I would be honored to step in and help guide you where he no longer can. I want to keep you, Josey, and your mom safe more than anything else in this world. Would you be alright with that? Will you let me help you keep your mom and sister safe?"

I try not to hold my breath as I wait but I need a positive answer. My mind races as I give him the time to consider my offer. Please don't make this harder. Let me in. I need you. I need your sister. I need your mother. I need the ones who now hold my heart.

"We can try. but if you make Mom or Josey cry, I'll kick your ass."

"If it's anything but happy tears I'll take everything you and your uncle give me without complaint." Raising my hand, I extend it out for him to shake. The moment the weight of his small hand settles in my heart nearly cracks from the happiness that rushes through me.

"You and I will always protect our family." I happily make the vow with my son to protect all that we hold dear between us.

"Speaking of family, why don't you go outside and find your uncle." With a light hand, she pushes our son in the direction of the opening. "And next time you decide to use that language I'll wash your mouth out with soap, young man."

"Tell Axel to come in here as well," I throw the words over my shoulder as I grip Ember's arm, alarmed by the paleness of her face now that I see her in the light of the fire. I keep my tone light so that I don't worry him.

I barely hear his acknowledgment as I gently pull my woman

closer. Her body leans heavily against my own without a fight. My arms now around her frame pick up the slightest tremors that roll through her body making my breath hitch.

"Ember… Moye malen'koye plamya, what is wrong?" Laying my forehead softly upon her's I nearly jerk back in shock. "Fuck, you're burning up, detka!"

"I don't feel so well, Mikhail." Her knees fall from under her as she gives a small whimper.

"Axel," I yell to the mouth of the cave as I scoop her into my arms and spin to the fire. As my knee hits the rocky floor a low moan whispers across my neck. Ember's head weakly rolls toward my chest. Her eyes stare dimly up at me causing my heart to drop. I call her name but get no response.

"What happened?" The medic drops beside me pulling out his light to see better.

"She was fine a minute ago talking with me before we came in here to see Hunter. She sent him out and when I looked up, she was pale but now she isn't responding to me."

I slam a wall down on my worry as I watch him rip open her coat. Blood stains more than half of her injured side. Fuck! Cupping her head, I lean down and lay my cheek against hers.

"Cold." Her body shudders harder than ever within my arms.

"I know, sladkaya. Give us just a few minutes, and we will get you warmed up." Kissing her head, I turn my eyes to watch Axel as he pulls her sweater from the gauze around her shoulder. There is no white visible, only red. Peeling the soaked wrapping back we both suck in harsh gasps.

"Fuck."

"Ember, when did you start feeling sick?" He doesn't take his eyes off her skin as he works.

"Don't know. Focused on finding Hunter." Her lashes flutter

180

on my cheek. "Didn't feel anything since the climb."

"Out of the mine?"

"Yeah." Her voice is fading fast.

His hands stills for a beat before driving into action. Ripping his pack from his back it thumps on the ground with his hands pulling things out before it even settles. Wiping the area clean to see the extent of the damage she inflicted on herself without thought to see our son's safe return.

"Ember, you ripped all the stitches out. The area around the hole is nearly shredded. I need you to stay as still as possible for me. I can't stitch this again so I'm going to wrap it as tight as you can stand. Can you do that for me?"

"'kay."

Axel's eyes flick up to my own as he pulls open the needle of morphine waiting for my permission to give it to her. I nod even as I clutch her closer at her weak protests to hold her still. I don't know how she can cause so much pain upon herself but remain silent in her torment. She may not think she needs it, but I don't allow her the opportunity to object. My woman is hurt, and she is going to get some relief from the pain even if she doesn't like it.

She doesn't utter a sound while he works on the slowly bleeding wound, but I feel every hitch of breath she tries to hide. "Almost done, moye plamya," I whisper over the shell of her ear. Her lips brush my neck in a soft kiss in answer and I smile for her.

"Alright the bleeding was almost done already, so keeping the gauze tight will get it stopped altogether rather quickly. Drink this." Pushing two pills past her lips, he holds the canteen up without giving her a choice. "I want this drained before you get any sleep."

"She will." Pulling her higher into my arms, I take the water and force it to her lips. It's not nearly the struggle I thought it would be to get it all in her. A few small trickles track down her throat. She chases the container when I pull it away.

"Rest now." Axel lays a hand on her head.

"Hunter."

"I'll get him for you." He stands but doesn't leave right away. "Get her comfortable for the night."

Grunting my acknowledgment, I reach for my own bag, pull out the survival blanket, and wrap it around her shivering frame. I maneuver her onto her good shoulder and lay her head on my bag before curling around her from behind.

A soft scrap of gravel brings my head up as Hunter drops in front of us. His eyes widen in fear as he takes her drained features in. Reaching out I take his hand in a firm grip to get his attention. "She will be fine, Hunter. She is just tired and needs some rest."

We lock our eyes, understanding what needs to be done without having to say another word. His throat works and his eyes tear up but not one falls. Even though his smile is watery he curls up against her front without complaint just as the rest of the team filters in. Ember reaches for him even in her exhausted state and pulls him close under the blanket. With him in her arms, she relaxes into me and falls asleep with a contented smile.

Viking makes his way to us. Without a word, he reaches into his pack and pulls out his own blanket to lay over his nephew and sister. Looks like both of us are going to have a cold night.

Chapter 30

My head is fuzzy and my body aches but I'm not the least bit worried or afraid. Comfort are the warmth surround me, the small body in my arms, and the large frame caging both of our bodies against their own. It's enough that I can push the discomfort away and feel the pull of sleep drag me down into a cozy dozing state.

My nose dips into the shaggy hair of my son's head and my arms tighten around him. Pain slams through my shoulder and I just keep the sound of pain from escaping my lips. Fire creeps around my arm but I force the pain away; willing myself to relax so that I don't wake either of the bodies pressed tightly to me.

"Shh…, Ember. You are safe," my Russian whispers in my ear.

I would laugh if everything didn't hurt so much. Releasing the tension brought on by the pain brings forth another more immediate problem. "I have to pee," I keep my voice just as low hoping not to wake my sleeping son.

His big body pulls away before he helps me untangle myself from the boy's hold. Shivers take hold as the cooler air hits me but don't last long. Gently he lifts me and carries me toward the entrance of our hiding spot. In a normal world I would demand that he put me down and let me walk on my own but after the day we've had I let him have his way. There are just times in a woman life that she has to let go of a certain level of pride.

My body aches enough that I know the walk out of here is going to leave me drained by the end of the day. I only need to be strong for a few more hours so that I don't worry everyone. As it is I'm going to have a gang of overprotective men and Hunter watching every move I make. This is going to be a trying day.

It's still dark out as we make our way into the cold past the thermal blanket that someone wedged into the opening to trap the heat inside. I'm thankful to be tucked in Mikhail's arms as he keeps his back to the wind and off me. I can just make out a man hiding in the shadows on watch. They give a nod as we make our way past.

Gradually he lets my feet touch the ground but refuses to let go. I don't even have a chance to reach for the buttons of my pants before he's kneeling down, popping the latch, pulling the zipper, and peeling them down my legs. My fleece thermals are next. The freezing wind chills my skin instantly, only to be chased away by his hands as they rub over the puckered flesh.

"I could have done that," I say though it comes out more teasing than annoyed. I really don't have the energy to argue with anyone over anything right now. I just don't have the drive to demand anything for myself if it isn't life or death. Not when I know what's ahead of us today.

"You are not to use that arm," His voice is laced with steel as he stares me down daring me to try anything. "Now pee so I can get you warmed up before we head out."

"So damn bossy."

A sharp slap on my ass rocks me forward as a low moan slips past my lips. Mikhail is immediately there catching me before I tip over with his arms rounding my waist and hugging me close as he looks up at me in concern. Now is not the time to want him to manhandle me but damn did that wake me up. Not the time or place girl, I internally scold myself.

"If you wanted me in your arms all you have to do is say so no need to get violent. You can hold me all you want once we get out of here." I drop my lips to the top of his head to hide the heat in my cheeks.

"No sass today Ember just let me take care of you." Blue eyes soften as they stare up at me from his lower position.

"Aren't I already doing that?"

"Plamya, please."

"Okay."

Once he rises to his feet it takes a bit of balance to take care of business. I let him help me get my pants back in place without a word of complaint. Of course, he won't allow me to walk by myself and I'm in the air before I get one word of difference in. He doesn't waste any more time as he heads for the warmth of the cave.

Setting me down by the coals of the fire he grabs the blanket he left on the ground and wraps it around my shoulders. His lips brush faintly over my hair before he disappears for a moment. Returning with smaller limbs, he airs the coals to get the flames going again.

Once the flames are burning hot, he sits behind me and wraps me close to him again. Since I stumbled back to the cabin, he hasn't been able to stop touching me at any small chance. It's like he thinks I'm a dream set to disappear if he isn't careful. Some times I can't help but feel the same way. The man seems too good to be real.

Next to us Hunter starts tossing back and forth for a second. I don't have a chance to do more than turn my head to watch him before his head settles into my lap. Smiling, I reach down and run my fingers through his hair. Gently separating the tangles so that I don't wake him. He's always been a strong mamma's boy. If there was ever a day that I got out of the house without him begging to go with me, I can't remember it. It never mattered if it was a school day or subzero out, he always wanted to follow me into the woods.

I can only be grateful now that he has always had so much interest in the land and animals that we make our living from. All the lessons he had to learn the hard way to be safe in these woods when he didn't want to listen to me. Every single endless question I had to find the patience to answer him as honestly as I could for his age. The teachings that my family handed down to me and I am teaching my children is what kept him safe in the face of the danger we find ourselves in.

Mikhail shifts behind me; his arm lowering to lay over Hunter's shoulders protectively. "You raised him well," his voice is a bare whisper in the air.

I can't answer past the lump of tears building in my throat so

I just nod knowing that he will feel it.

"Let's get everyone up so we can go collect our daughter," Mikhail plants a kiss on my cheek with a husky whisper before climbing to his feet to get the guys moving.

Axel heads over and pulls my clothes down to see if the gauze needs to be changed. I put up with the poking and prodding refusing to show any pain so that we can just get moving. He must be satisfied with what he sees. He pushes more pills between my lips and forces another canteen into my hands.

Grumbling Hunter tries to curl back up and bury his head into my stomach. "Come on buddy it's time to get moving."

"Have to?"

"Yeah, buddy we need to get back to your sister. Get my bag for me please."

"Kay," he mumbles slowly rolling off me to do what I ask.

I wave off what the group tries to share with us and go for the jerky still stashed in the pack. My guts churn as the venison hits it threatening to send it back the way it came but I force it down and hope none of the guys are watching too closely. I'm going to need all the strength packed into the strips of meat.

"Mom?"

"Yeah baby?"

"Are you okay?"

A soft snort escapes as I try to hold in my humor. "I'm good Hunter, just ready to head home."

Strong arms wrap around me from behind and snag the piece of meat from my hand and a soft bag of warm oats is pushed into my finger. Damn Russian I roll my eyes with a sigh but finish the small portion without saying anything. They go down easier than my jerk thankfully but my body still isn't into eating. Even if my guts aren't happy with me, I should eat more but I don't think I'll be able to keep much down. Holding the bag up I offer more of my food grateful he isn't trying to force me to eat more than I can stand right now.

"Are you warm enough, Hunter?" Mikhail looks over the clothes he has on with a critical eye.

"Yes, sir," Hunter doesn't seem to know what else he should call Mikhail.

"Hunter, we are family. You do not need to call me sir. I will break my neck looking for my father if you continue to use that term," He tries to sound stern but even Hunter can hear the humor in his voice.

"Yes, sir," Hunter grins eyeing up the man.

Growling the big man darts forward and tackles my son sending them both to the floor. Poor kid doesn't stand a chance as Mikhail begins tickling him, but he tries. He kicks his feet out recklessly in an attempt to connect with some small part of the man. He refuses to laugh challenging him to do his worst and he sure delivers as he adjusts to reach Hunter's ribs. One stroke. Two and Hunter howls under determined fingers.

"Enough children we don't need to wake the whole mountain," I mock scowl from my spot by the fire but seeing Mikhail be so free with my son has my eyes stinging.

Gritting my teeth to keep the pain from showing, I shift and start to stand up. There's no time to sit around. If we don't start moving soon, I'm not going to have the will power to keep going. My shoulder feels like someone is driving a red-hot poker into the wound and twisting it at every single violent angle imaginable. It's amazing what adrenaline allows your body to dismiss cause fuck it hurts.

I'm not even halfway to my feet when Mikhail's hands are on me; lifting me up and setting me on my feet. His warm body pressing into my back allowing me a moment to gather myself. He doesn't push or demand anything; he simply waits for me to take the time I need to ready myself.

"Hunter, can you carry your mother's bag?"

"I can take it," I grumble reaching for it with my good arm.

"I've got it, Mom." He backs away with a scowl.

The leather is over his shoulders before I can say anything else, so I just let it happen. "Thanks baby."

"Time to head out is everyone ready?" Joe wraps his arm around Hunter's shoulders as he comes to stand with us.

"Yeah, let's get out of here. I'm ready to get back to Josey," I smile forcing the pain away. Lord I can't wait to see my little girl. I need to get home and hold my family in my arms.

Chapter 31

We haven't hiked for more than an hour when I notice the first slips of Ember's mask. Her lips thin; face white and growing paler with each step she takes. Leather-covered shoulders bowing under the strain of her pain. She isn't going to last long enough to march the whole way back to our rides.

Letting Hunter with her, I hurry to Viking at the front of the line. "Call Irish in now," I growl as low as possible so no one else hears us.

He casts a look over his back as we shift to the left to follow the faint ridge line trail down. "Fuck! I was hoping she'd make it just a little further, but she's hurt a hell of a lot more than Axel or us figured. I wish so would stop being so stubborn and tell us how bad off she is. Keep her moving. There's a spot ten minutes from here with enough clearance for him to set down."

Grunting I make my way back to her side. I stay closer than before as worry chews at my bones. I can hear the effort her lungs are making as she fights for breath. She must have a cracked or busted rib with the harshness of her sawing lungs. Damn it we're too far out for the help she needs and we can't stop. Dear Father, please give us the strength to help her. Amen.

Her face is pinched from the pain she is in, but nothing else gives away just how much she's hurting. Even though she looks nearly white from the strain of our movements, she keeps moving. Sensing my gaze, she looks at me with a soft smile. Even the slight twitch of her mouth leaves a flash of pain in her eyes. I don't know if she can physically make it to the clearing her brother has in mind.

Several times I swear she is about to stumble but she always keeps her feet under her. No matter how many times, it seems like I'm going to have to reach over and catch her; she always regains her feet. The footing is getting worse as is my agitation at the helpless situation that I cannot make better for her. Her foot catches on a snow-covered rock causing her to stumble sideways and I lunge for her. She's so tired, not even a whisper of pain escapes her pale lips. Her complexion is far whiter than I've ever seen on another living human.

My heart clenches in near panic as I slide my arm under her good one to keep her up. She nearly loses control and lets her body fall against me. I adjust my grip quickly to her hip to hold her steady. She hangs slack in my arms as her body shakes from exertion. A barely there cry leaves her lips at the way she meets my body. True fear is trying to take over but I call on my demons to push it away. They bear their fangs unwilling to lose her.

"You can't keep this up, Ember, why must you always fight to appear strong?" I whisper into the fur of her hat, holding her close to share some of my body heat.

A hand on my shoulder has my neck snapping around to see Maskin. Nodding he pulls the straps of my pack off for me. Slinging it over the top of his own he moves forward to give me a moment.

"Sorry." I can barely hear her words as I pull her shivering form closer rubbing my hands rapidly up and down her back. "All I know."

"Ember." It's all I can get out around the choke hold on my voice. Pulling her closer I bury my face in her shoulder and lay light kisses on the exposed skin. "No more of this do you hear me?"

Not giving her a chance to answer I change my hold to swing her up into my arms. The leather does a decent job of padding her to lay against me comfortably. Her face buries itself into my shoulder to cover the whimpers of pain my movement send through her.

"Hold on we're getting out of here." Kissing her head, I promise her before starting forward again.

Normally her weight wouldn't affect my movements in the slightest, but the snow is slowly melting. Each step I take has to be placed just right or both of us are going to be on the ground and I refuse to allow her any more pain. She hurts enough as she is even though she's still trying to hide it from everyone by pressing into my shoulder.

Hunter doesn't say a word, just moves closer to my side. His sad eyes take in his mother in my arms before he puts on a tough face just like Ember and faces ahead. Every once in a while, he'll dart in front of me to show me the best path. Damn he moves just like his mother.

It isn't long before the cutting of blades through the air signals that Irish has found us. We make it into the clearing just as he's setting down. The sleek black body of the bird is a welcome sight as we make our way closer. "Always there," I whisper as she groans.

Viking grabs Hunter's head to keep him low of the whooping blades as they rush forward and yank the door open so that we can all climb in. The team all stay back as I climb in with Ember still curled into my arms. Axel follows as Viking lifts Hunter into the seat next to me.

More bodies crowd into the space. It's going to be a tight fit to get everyone on, but we've been in worse positions. Reaching over I slid my son closer to my side to give the others more room. He settles against me without hesitation; leaning close to get nearer to his mother. His small hand sliding into her. She gives he a weak squeeze barely able to keep hold of his fingers.

The sight of bodies remaining outside of the bird has me on edge. Viking and his team stand outside with grim faces. I yell to be heard over the roaring of the engine, "what are you doing?"

"Take care of them! She's A+. I'm going to get my parents and Josey. We'll meet you there." Viking leans in to slap my shoulder with a hard look. He pulls out to close the door before I can argue against them staying on their own.

Irish lifts us before I can do anything. I understand why he's staying. If I did not have Ember in my arms and Hunter by my side, I'd still be in the woods hunting the fuckers who dared to touch my family.

"I need to see her shoulder. Can you move on your mom's other side and hold her feet up for me?" Axel shifts closer and kneels down on the floor.

"Move down but keep her head in your lap." He shrugs out of his outer gear as I move her how he wants her.

Gently as I'm able in the moving craft I lift her off of me and slide close to the door. I lay her across the seat with her feet on our son and her head cradled in my arms as I lean down to cut off her view of what Axel is doing.

"Mom's gonna be okay, right?" Hunter's voice is strained.

I turn my head and send him my most reassuring smile. Reaching over I cup the back of his head and give him a gentle squeeze. "Our girl is going to be just fine son."

Chapter 32

During the thirty-minute air trip, I push out negative thoughts and focus on my woman's pulse beating under my palm and holding our son's hand with the other. He'd slipped his hand into mine not long after we took off. He spent the trip keeping a sharp eye on every move Axel makes as he worked on her. I'm not sure how she is conscious.

At her first low cry of pain, she grabs my hand as it stokes over her chest and down her stomach. My eyes dart to our boy but he's not looking at me. His eyes are glued to what is happening with his mother. Tears glint in his eyes and his lips begin to tremble. I give his small fingers a squeeze and hold onto him as long as he will allow.

Below us I see the medical team waiting for on the roof watching as we drop lower to land. As soon as the skids touch the pavement someone yanks the door open before jumping out. The rest of my team follows, leaving Axel, Hunter and I holding Ember as the doctors rush forward.

Gently we lift her into the waiting hands of the staff. Her hair long pulls from its braid in wild breeze created by the rotors. Arms lay limply at her sides as they settle her on the gurney. Blood has seeped from the latest dressing. She's strapped in quickly as they rush her to the doors.

Jumping down I turn to help my son. He stands on the edge of the door and lets me lift him down. Once on his feet he refuses to let go of my hand again as we step away from the bird. Maybe I don't have as much work to do as I feared in getting him to trust me.

Two more doctors hurry forward eyes intent on my son. "Let us have him." The female reaches for him with a frown.

"Stay away from me!" Hunter jerks away from her to hide behind me; eyes wide and full of unease.

The demons who had settled into a quiet watch, come to the front with a roar in reaction to the agitation of fear in his voice. I drop and pull him up into my arms protectively to keep from spills blood. "I've got you." I whisper as his arms hug my neck in a choke hold.

"Sir I need to look at the boy. Please set him down." The lady strides forward again with a deeper scowl twisting her lips.

"Back off! Can't you see how scared he is?" My words rumble out like thunder causing the men around me to lay hands over weapons. This lady doesn't want to keep testing me when I'm already so on edge.

"Mikhail, calm yourself." Ilya grips my arm with a look of warning.

Gritting my teeth I keep the cage in place and wave my men down. "They just took his mother in now get out of my way."

"Sir, if you are not his father, I'll need you to hand the boy over so I can do my job." Her hand lands on her hip as she demands I hand him over with the other with an impatient finger wag..

"Dad, I want mom!" Hunter cries into my neck as he locks his feet around my sides.

My heart's spasm nearly drops me to my knees when he calls me Dad. I don't know if he means it, or if he is so scared, he doesn't want to leave my arms. I sure as hell don't care which way he means as I hold him closer, but this woman will not take my son from my arms.

"I already examined the boy, and he is with his father. Now get out of our way." Axel shoulders between us as my men surround me, a wall of pure muscle and threat. Thank God he was able to talk because I'm not sure I can right now.

"Doctor Bloom! Axel has the boy covered you're needed in the ward stat!" Nurse Everly's dark curls appear from the elevator as she runs towards us before the woman can say anything else. "Mr. Solokov, we have the room ready for you and the team."

"Thank you Everly, please have some hot food sent up. We are all quite hungry." Ilya steps up with a smile grateful to the woman for defusing the situation with a clearly new doctor on staff.

"We already have your order in; it should be up shortly. We'll let you know when she comes out of surgery." She smiles, leaving us to make our own way to the room as she and Dr. Bloom angrily whisper between themselves while they jog out of sight.

Hunter still refuses to let go of me, so I carry him into the building enjoying the weight of him in my arms. His head rests on my shoulder as we make our way down the halls. Another piece of my soul fits into place. Now, I just need to hold my whole family.

It doesn't take us long to reach the private room that is always on standby for us with Axel leading the way. Seven single bunks line the green wall to the south with our storage units sitting by the head of each one. A thin oval table stands before the window to the east. This room will never see anyone but our team. No one can get in without being coded into our system as well as a pass code that changes every few hours.

"Ilya." I nod to the boy. My second pulls a phone from his locker to do as I order without asking any questions.

Kneeling at the foot of my normal bed, I pull Hunter's arms from around my neck. He allows me to stand him before me so that I can strip from all my weather gear and body armor. His eyes never leave me the entire time. His lips tremble slightly but he's back to hiding his fear.

"Desyat' minut, ser,." Ilya lets me know as he begins taking off his own gear.

"Let's get cleaned up so we don't look like we rolled in the trash when your mother gets back." I hold out my hand so that we can head for the shower.

"I don't have any clothes." He doesn't take my hand right away but frowns up at me.

"You will by the time we get done."

"How?"

"Magic."

"I'm ten, not four, sir." If he rolled his eyes any harder, he would probably lose his head. Dimitri is going to love this boy if only to watch Vlad come undone at the eye rolls. Our older brother hates them.

"What does age have to do with magic?" Squatting down, I lower my voice but speak loud enough that his silent guard can hear me from his bunk. "Maskin never takes his pendent off because he believes it keeps him from being seen while he is hunting."

I watch his eyes dart behind me to the man in question. He must believe whatever he sees because he grabs my hand. The rest of the team are looking forward to getting cleaned up, but they stay in the main room while we go first. Just as I told him the clothes are waiting for him before he steps out of the stall.

Food is on the table for us when we come back out. "Go eat." I nod to the table where the team sits waiting for us.

As we're eating a knock sounds on the door. Alexie sitting next to the door gets up to answer it. Everyone stops eating and shifts in their seats waiting to see who comes in.

Everly steps into the room with a smile. "Mr. Sokolov, she is out of surgery and on her way up. She lost quite a bit of blood but she's a fighter. I just wanted to let you know that both mother and child are doing well."

"Child?" I stand and make my way to wait in front of her wondering if I heard her wrong.

"I'm sorry I thought you knew from how protective you are of her. Your wife is eleven weeks along but hasn't woken up yet, so we haven't been able to get any other information from her yet."

"Pregnant?" The word is a mere whisper of sound as I stare at her in disbelief. The entire room has gone silent. I can feel the men's eyes on my back. "She never said anything."

"Um yes sir. Babies are tricky, some mothers don't realize they're carrying until after twelve weeks but it's not common. Well, I just wanted to update you. The doctor will be up shortly to tell you everything." With a smile, she's out the door before I can form any other thoughts. Pregnant!

Hunter's hand slipping into mine rips me from my stupor with frightening speed as I drop to my knees next to him. "Has she been sick at all the last few weeks? Think very carefully." I grip his shoulders so he can see how serious my question is.

"No sir. She's been herself other than being happier."

Before I can ask more the door opens and the doctor rolls in the bed that my woman rests in. They roll her into the closed medical room and get her comfortable. I.V. lines are hung, and machines are hooked up before they leave her to rest.

"Hunter, why don't you go check on your mom?" The words aren't fully out of my mouth before he darts into the room and climbs in the chair to get closer to her. He's careful not to climb on the bed as I'm sure he wants to.

"Mr. Sokolov, she lost a lot of blood so we will watch her closely for the next few days but given everything that she's been through she has come out far better than she should have. Your wife is very lucky. When she wakes up, we'll have a better picture of how to move forward. Until then just keep her comfortable." He lays a hand on my shoulder.

"The baby?" My voice is hoarse and I'm barely able to get the words out.

"Just fine. As much as Momma went through it amazingly

hasn't affected the child in any way that we can see."

"Thank you."

I have my spare phone in hand before the doctor is fully out the door. As always, they answer on the first ring when I call. "I'm calling in my favor," I say before stepping further from the men as I talk.

Hanging up, I walk into the room and close the curtain; shutting my family in what little privacy the room offers. Hunter leans on her good shoulder holding her hand as he watches me. The lost look in his eyes has me moving forward. Lifting him up I sink on the bed before slipping him onto my lap. Together, we recline on the raised bed so that both of us can wrap our arms around her sleeping figure. Time slips by as we hold her.

"She's going to be okay right?" His voice pleads for me to make her wake up so that he can hear it from her too.

"She's going to be just fine. All of us will be." I promise; reaching across him to lay my hand on her still-flat tummy. Now that we are safe the new firmness under my hands is noticeable. The place where our next child rests. Fuck how did this happen. If we hadn't shown up what would happen to her and the children?

"Why did you call her your wife?"

"Because she is. We may not have said it in front of a priest yet but God, heard us. Just as you are my son. We made a commitment to be together to each other."

He does not seem to know what to make of my words, so he changes the subject. "I'm gonna be a big brother again."

"Yes, son you are. Do you think the two of us can keep your mother, Josey, and the baby out of trouble?"

"Do you love mom?"

"With everything in me son but I don't just want your mom. I want all of you."

"You're gonna love your baby more than me and Josey." He keeps his gaze locked on his hands. It's not hard to hear the sadness in his voice and it makes me see red. Who the hell put those thoughts in my son's head?

"Look at me, Hunter." Just like his mother, he turns further away from me, but I am not letting him do that to us. "Hunter."

Cupping his head, I make him turn to see how serious I am. "You and your sister may not be my blood, but you will always be mine. You are my son, my child, and you just like your sister have my heart just as much as your mother and your new sibling. Do you know why?"

"Why?"

Pushing his hair away from his eyes I lean down touching our heads without letting go of his gaze. "Because we are a family. As soon as your uncle gets here with the rest of the group we are going to go home where there will be even more family waiting to meet you."

"How big is the family?"

"Well, you have us your mother's parents, my parents, my three brothers, your uncles that are in the next room, and your uncle Joe is bringing your other uncles."

Familiar hazel eyes stare back at me as his mouth hangs wide open. "Wow."

"Yes, son. Now do you think we can handle the trouble our girls are going to send our way?"

"Mom doesn't like being told what to do. If this baby comes out like her, we're going to be in a lot of trouble."

All I can do is laugh because that sounds far too accurate to be a lie. Ember has always been a fighter. Hell, that is what drew me to her in the first place. I still dream about the look on her face before I stepped in.

"I'll tell you a secret son. The best women are the fighters. Ones who make you be better. Ones that make sure you hold on to what you say and do just so you don't disappoint them. The ones you work to please because making them smile is the best gift they can give you. Your mother is that kind of woman."

"How do you know?"

Ruffling his hair, my eyes travel along Ember's face. "When you find the right one, they will fight with you, not against you."

Chapter 33

Fucking hospitals how I hate you all. I hate waking up in these nasty places. I am glad that my two guys are talking and not paying attention to me. It gives me a few moments to lay here and take in everything that's happening.

It doesn't seem real. There have been no symptoms. No morning sickness. I haven't even felt my jeans become too tight. I never thought I would go through the journey again. I was content with the card's life tossed my way.

Guess God is having a good laugh at my plans right now. Damn Russian romantic. I don't have the energy for tears no matter how much I want to cry. Fighting my way out of sleep and now having a talk with Mikhail is about all I'm up for today.

"I remember all the trouble you give me young man." My voice feels heavy and slightly slurred from the induced sleep. Waking up to my guys beside me is the best feeling in the world. The only thing that's missing is my baby girl.

"Mom you're okay!" His small body spins to latch onto my neck. "I love you mom."

"Love you more baby." My eyes sink tiredly as I roll my head to rest on top of his.

"Hunter, will you go have Axel call the doctor." Mikhail pats his back to get him moving.

"'Kay!" He's off the bed and out the door yelling for the medic. The men are quick to calm him down and engage him so that we can have a few moments to ourselves. Axel smiles and leaves the room as my silent shadow lays a calming hand on the boy's shoulder.

"Embe, Moye plamya." Mikhail's hands feather over my checks to dig into my messy hair. That shit needs to be washed with all the grim I can feel scratching my scalp. I wonder if I can get him on board with a shower?

"You have taken far too many years off my life in the last few days." He kisses me as we both smile lip to lip.

"Keeps life interesting you know. Kinda like how, I'm gonna have another kid and we're suddenly married. Must have slept through the ceremony."

"The only surprises I want are ones like this little miracle." His hand joins the mine as it lays on top of my middle because that arm is strapped to my chest. "You are my wife; we just have to sign the paperwork. I told you I was not letting you go."

"Didn't say I was opposed to the idea of being tied down again. Wondering what my new name is all of a sudden is all. How the hell do we have a baby on the way? I know that we used protection."

"I am not sure how either, but I am not sorry."

"Oh, great you're going to be a helicopter dad, aren't you? Kids won't stand a chance."

"Ember-Lee Jessica Anderson Russell Sokolov if you were not in a hospital bed, I would paint your ass red with my hand."

"Is that a promise? I'm sure I've got enough energy to get up." Lord have mercy, I love that growly voice of his.

"Don't think about it. Maybe when you are healed up." Way to get a girl's hopes up.

"I can make that happen."

"Tease." As much as he tries to hold back the amusement in the vibrations still send shivers down my spine.

"You know this is the second baby who's decided to tell me they're coming when I end up in the hospital. Not sure what kinda odds that leaves us with." My words are slurring more with each word. I sound drunk without even one of the fun benefits that come with booze. God, I'm tired. "What kind of mom am I?"

"The best kind. Now no more bad thoughts." His warm lips trail over my face until I have to give a few tired laughs. The warmth of his skin slowly makes its way into mine chasing away the internal chill that refuses to leave my system anytime I ever think about a hospital. Maybe I can just make him hug me until they let me out of this death trap. Oops sorry this wonderful place of healing. Gag!

"You need sleep Ember."

"Not yet. Just hold me please." I don't want him to let go of me. Not now. Not ever. How did this man bind my heart up so quickly?

"Easily, moye plamya. Ty moye serdtse." Having him hold me in his arms, fingers mindlessly combing through my hair, and whispering in Russian is the only thing that matters in the silence of this room.

Not ten minutes later, the doctor knocks before coming in. He's younger than I thought he would be. Maybe early forties if I had to offer a guess and thin glasses perch on the bottom of his nose.

"Mrs. Sokolov, I'm Dr. Wolfe. How are you feeling?"

"Better than I probably look."

"On a scale of one to ten, what would you say your pain is at just now?" He eyes the readings on the machines while still giving me his attention.

"Whatever answer she tells you, triple it." Joe marches into the room with water dripping from his hair to soak his clean shirt. "If you've heard of the farmer pain scale, that's what you use on her. She's got a huge pain tolerance."

"I don't need to get up to trounce your ass peanut brain. I know the magic word. I feel fine doc at the most a two, just weak."

"Well with the amount of blood you lost that's to be expected. You're not due for another pain pill for another few hours but let us know if the pain starts to worsen."

"Don't need them." I don't need my eyes open to see the disapproval on Mikhail's face.

"Ember I think.."

"Don't Mikhail." I don't let him get any further. My tones

make it clear that this is a line he doesn't want to cross with me. He wisely closes his mouth.

"Mrs. Sokolov you do realize that you have a hole in your shoulder, a concussion, and three fractured ribs that nearly pierced your lung? On top of the damage from your injuries adding the stress of this level of pain is not good for the baby."

"Yep. I'm fine." I open my eyes to stare down my brother. He's about to lose his mind. Face red, fists clenched, and veins pulsing in his neck. Everyone goes completely silent, even the others in the adjoining room. Dr. Wolfe's lips move without a sound as he stares at me. I don't know what his problem is, I haven't grown another head. I don't need or want his pills.

"As your doctor, I can't say that I approve of your refusal. None of the medications will affect the baby. If that is your concern then I promise they are perfectly safe."

"No meds." Mikhail is quiet beside me, but the worry is pouring off his frame. His fingers lace through mine as he moves closer. None of them can understand why I'm refusing but his silent acceptance of my choice keeps me steady.

"Ember please think about this." Joe steps up to the foot of the bed and grabs my foot.

"Joesph your sister said no. Listen to her or get out." Mom snaps storming through the curtain. Her hands plant themselves on her hips as she glares up at him.

"Don't be pigheaded about this! She's in pain and has the ability to get help to manage it. Why are you refusing?" He refuses to look at Mom thinking he can get me to back down. That's a mistake and he dang well knows it.

"Out young man." Mom's first and only warning.

"Not until she tells me!" He still won't look away from me as I continue to refuse to answer him.

"Out of this room right now. I will not have you bully her into things." Her palm connects with his backside repeatedly until she chases him out.

Then she comes back to glare at the doctor. "Anything else you have to say?"

"I'll be around to check on you in a while." He nods at Mikhail before walking out.

Her gaze lands on the man next to me. "I will only say this." She levels a finger at him. "If you hurt my girl and grand babies there will be no place on God's green earth that you can hide from me. I'll make what your team can do look like child's play."

"You will be one in a long line of those after my life if anything were to ever happen mam. If something I do causes Ember or our children pain, I will hand her my blade to do with as she wishes."

"Good boy." She laughs giving his cheek a pat before walking out.

Once we're alone he turns back to me. "I will not push but please tell me why you are refusing the pills."

"I don't want to talk about it. All I will say is that losing Jackson put me in a dark place."

He holds my gaze before nodding. "Alright."

"Mommy!!" The fireball flies into the run and straight to Mikhail's side. "Up Kail. Up!"

"Come here, Milaya." He has her in his arms before the words are even finished. Blue eyes swim as he takes her in. The man is already a goner. Looks like I'm going to have to be the bad guy.

She plops down in his lap and wraps an arm around his head so she can lean over to whisper in my ear. "He promised to save you, mommy."

"He's good at that baby girl." I look over the top of her head to share a smile with the man.

Chapter 34

Two days of being isolated in this hospital room and I'm about to lose my mind. I don't mind the nurse and doctor coming to check on Ember. They are doing their job and being respectful about it. They take what she tells them as fact and no longer try to push her.

No, that isn't my problem. My problem happens to be six foot and two hundred fifty pounds of pissed off overprotective brother. If he isn't playing with the children, he is standing over my woman fuming that she is still refusing to take any pain medication. I'm afraid if he comes in to start anything today, I might end up bloodying my children's uncle in front of them. It doesn't take a genius to figure out why she is refusing.

Only her mother and father know the full reason why she keeps refusing the pills, but they aren't saying anything. I won't say anything. Viking has all but thrown a tantrum demanding answers. My mother-in-law just sends a glare at him, and he stops for a time. She's also the only reason that Viking hasn't blown up and killed me for getting Ember pregnant.

"Kail, when can we leave? I'm bored." Josey keeps her voice muted because Ember is sleeping with the little girl lying across the foot of the bed with her head hanging off the edge.

"Well, we can't have that now can we little trouble maker?" Viking steps in pulling one of her curls. "The doctor is here to see Mommy, so you and Hunter are gonna come with me to get some lunch from the cafeteria. The nurse told me they have chocolate cake today and I'm craving something gooey."

"Can I have cake, Kail?"

"Josephine Ann it's not even ten. No cake." Ember opens an eye to glare at them.

"But mommy!!" That little lip wobbles as she turns those pleading eyes my way. Even Hunter look to me hopefully.

"You heard your mother, Milaya. It's too early for cake." No way am I falling for that pout while Ember slides the same look her mother uses straight to me.

We get to go home today, and I want to sleep next to my woman in a bed that has enough room to comfortable fit my entire family. I've slept with only half my body on the narrow bed next to my woman and kids every night. It's the only way either of us can really rest easily.

As much as my in-laws and Viking have tried to move the children we refuse to force the issue. All it took from either of them was a sad eye or pouty lip for me to allow them to stay with us. Am I a pushover for our kids? Yes. Am I still going to keep them close now that they are safe? Also, yes. Do I care that others don't approve? Fuck no I want them with me as much as possible.

"Alright, no cake for the munchkins and extra for me. Let's go trouble." Scooping her up he rushes them out the door. The three of them cackle in whispers they think we can't hear.

The door slams as Ember and I turn to each other. "I am sorely tempted to let him keep those two so he can experience the horrors they will dish out when that sugar wears off."

"Off one slice of cake, moye plamya?" A strand of that honeyed hair falls into her eyes as she tilts her head to ask me if I'm serious. Leaning in I hover over the warm beautiful face of the woman who has become my world and tug the strand.

"There's a reason we don't use sugar in our house. I'm letting you all deal with the fallout." That sassy grin pulls her lips just like our second night together. She's going to enjoy the show that follows but I'm not sure I will.

"Let them have this one day." Those full lips part to meet my own in a slow dance. All our heat and passion spill over with each small touch. There is no rush. No need to push for more. Both of us are content with this one simple touch.

"Knock. Knock." Dr. Wolfe steps into the room. "Are you ready to get out of here?"

"Hell yes!" Her eyes brighten. God, she lights up the world with that smile. "Clear me now, doc, 'cause I'm ready to bust out of this joint just to get some peace."

The man finally chuckles. "I already have the paperwork

started for you. Before you go, I thought you would like to do an ultrasound to see the baby. Give both of you some peace of mind."

"Yes! Let us see our little one." Her slim fingers lace with mine for a tight squeeze at my quick response as she holds back her laughter.

My heart feels as if it could explode as I watch them bring in the ultrasound equipment and set it up. The heel of my left foot hanging off the bed starts bouncing as we wait. A large glob of gel is dumped on her stomach before the wand is lowered to run over her skin.

Left, right, down, and up it goes before coming to a stop. Fast-whooshing rhythmic thuds fill the air making the nurse smile. "That is a strong heartbeat for the little one. Now let's see if they will stay still so I can get some measurements."

My eyes stay on the black and white image on the screen transfixed by the growing realization that we are seeing our child for the first time together. The best of both of us sheltering beneath my woman's ribs.

"Would you like to know the gender?" The nurse turns her eyes our way.

"You can tell this early?" I feel like I'm stumbling over my tongue to get the words out.

"Baby's just at twelve weeks, so yes."

I pull my eyes from the image of our child to look at my woman. "What do you want to do, moya lyubov'?"

"I made that choice by myself twice before. What do you want, Mikhail? Do you want to know?" Her eyes don't leave the image on the screen.

While her smile is sad her eyes are bright. Fuck! She went through this both times without Jackson. First with

Hunter because he was deployed and Josey because he was dead. Touching our heads, I cup both of her cheeks. Our eyes lock as I get lost in her beautiful hazel lights. They hold all her thoughts. She's strong enough to do this without me. It might tear her apart, but she would pull through it.

"I will be by your side for all our babies. Each and every single one will know both of us from the very beginning." It's a promise a man in my position can't make with any certainty but I do so anyway. Fuck, I'll quit and take us into hiding in the farthest reaches of the Russian frontier to keep my family safe.

"Okay." Hope burns bright behind the tears clouding those blue and green swirls.

With a kiss to her temple, I turn back to the nurse. "Who will we be welcoming into our family?"

"Let's see here." She swirls the wand for a moment before stopping with a smile. "You have one of each already don't you, mamma?"

"Yes."

"Well, it looks like daddy's going to have another little princess."

Chapter 35

We leave in a gray Land Rover with Mikhail's team spread out between two other non-descript cars. I don't fight Mikhail as he takes charge. This is his world and I have to trust him to get us out safely.

Also moving around so much after spending the last three days in bed is kicking my ass. I should have been up and moving the next day, but the boys demanded that I let them coddle me. My body is stiff, and sore given that I should have been up and around the next day. Not my first time with busted ribs.

Joe took his men and left in the helicopter that brought us in.

I'm glad he left with our parents. I need some time away from his constant watch, though I will miss having Mom around when everything is so up in the air. I love my brother and would throw down for him, but we need space. We aren't who we were the last time we saw each other.

I spend the ride dozing against Mikhail's shoulder with the kids strapped between us. Josey bouncing in her seat wakes me up as the car pulls to a stop. The team and another group surround the car facing out.

Mikhail gives us a smile and opens the door causing the men to move back to make room as he helps the kids out. Hunter latches on to Maskin's side and Josey jumps right into Ilya's arms. The big softie hugs her close, smiling over at me.

Mikhail ducks back in and I let him scoop me up to lift me out of the vehicle. "This is my brother Vlad; our Pakhan's home. We will be safe here until we agree on where to go."

"You make me sound argumentative."

"Moye plamya, watching you fight makes me…" He stops himself when he sees the kids turn our way. "But I will not fight about our family's safety. You are lucky I don't have us on a plane heading to my father's home in Russia already."

"Glad to know we have an understanding already." My eyes take in the sprawling house. Large thick blocks are stacked at least three stories high. A wall just as high surrounds the house and acres of kept land. At least I got the full story before getting dropped into the house.

As we pass through the doors, two men step off the last step of the sweeping stairs in front of us. Everything from hair color, style, build, and movements are the same. The only two differences are one is clean-shaven and smiling while the other has a trimmed beard and looks like he has a stick sticking up his ass.

"Brat." The one with the beard walks forward laying his hand on Mikhail's shoulder. "It lightens my heart to see you home unharmed." A small lift of his lips.

"Thank you for trusting my choice."

A darker shade of Mikhail's blue eyes sweeps over my body. "When have you ever given, me cause to doubt your choices before brat? Welcome to my home sister. Anything you or the children need all you must do is say so and it will be done."

"Thank you." Do I call him sir? Brother? Best leave it basic for now.

He gives me a nod before his gaze settles on the kids as they come in with the rest of the team. "You have full access to all areas of the house except those that my men are standing outside of. You are safe here, moya sem'ya."

His eyes flick over the kids, and me again before he turns to head down the hall to our right. "Once they are settled, come to the office, Mikhail." He disappears through the darkened hallway.

"Da, brat." he says, to his brother's back before the other one steps close.

"It is good to have you home, little brother." I watch in amusement as he flips his hand over my man's hair. All he can do is grumble since he hasn't let me down yet.

"Mommy? Kail?" Josey grips Ilya's neck as he comes to stand beside us. Her bottom lip wobbling in uncertainty. She wants to be in my man's arms but is not comfortable with so many strange men around. She may be an outgoing child, but she hates crowds just as much as I do.

The big man smiles far too brightly completely forgetting about us as he takes her in. "Da, Mikhail you are right. She is

Milaya. Welcome to our home, little one. I am your dyadya, Dimitri."

Surprisingly, when he holds his arms out for her, she pauses only briefly before easily slipping into them. "What does dyadya mean?" She leans back, studying his face. "He looks like you, Kail."

Laughing he tosses her up and catches her. "No, little, one he looks like dyadya Vlad and I. Come Milaya. Plemyannik you too. Let's get you something to eat while your mama gets settled in their room."

Maskin pushes Hunter after the laughing man carrying our little girl away. "Mama i Nikolay budet doma cherez neskol'ko chasov. Ona poshla za pokupkami dlya detey." He yells," he yells over his shoulder making Mikhail groan.

"That one is going to be trouble, isn't he?" I make sure to whisper just loud enough for the rest of the team I know to hear but not the men who are new.

Mikhail and Ilya laugh while the others lightly chuckle or try to hold it in. "He has his moments. Let me get you up to our room and comfortable before the chaos ascends on us."

"I thought Joe wasn't coming here for a while," I can't help but groan in annoyance. Growling, tossing my head over his arm nearly ready to kick my feet in frustration.

"No Ember. My mother will be here soon. We will have no quiet while she is here. I will have little time with you before she takes over the house." We start up the steps two at a time as he mumbles under his breath. The men still below make their way out of sight before I can ask any of them anything.

He stops at a door, and I twist it open before he can say anything. His foot kicks behind him shutting us in the room.

I don't get put on the bed like, I think. Instead, he keeps me close in his arms as he climbs onto the mattress. I don't know how he does it but the man moves me on the bed so he can hold me from behind without making my ribs burn any more than they already are.

"Moye plamya, I need to hold you." His big strong arms hug me close even as he watches the amount of pressure they put on my ribs. "I have needed you next to me these past months. You were all that I could think about. You drove me to distraction every day. I did not think I would ever hold you in my arms again. I was sure of it."

"Hmm feels better than I remember. I'm glad we don't have to rely on our memories anymore." A quick shimmy has every part of me flush with my big man. My body might be holding a silent rebellion, but lying here with him makes me feel far more relaxed than I have in years.

"I don't want to leave and meet with my brothers. I finally have you all to myself in my bed."

"So, stay."

Chapter 36

I have never been so bored out of my everlasting mind in my entire life. Promising Mikhail that I wouldn't leave the bed for anything, but the bathroom is totally biting me in the ass. If I wasn't so damn sore, I wouldn't have agreed so easily. Why am I still following his orders? It's been five hours, he better be grateful I lasted this long.

Waking up crowded by him and the kids without being flattened for the first time in days was a huge mood booster. After some light grumbling at the early wake up call from the kids, he got them up and out for the day.On his way out the door, he gave me a kiss, and a new cell phone. He wanted me to have a way to get a hold of him or the family if I need anything. Ten minutes of poking around on it is more than enough for me. It got tossed to the side without a second thought.

A soft knock on the door pulls me back to the present. I don't care who it is I'll welcome the distraction. "Come in."

"I brought you lunch." An older woman steps into the room. She might be slightly smaller than me but she is in decent shape. A few gray hair line the front of her dark hair. "The boys are still in the middle of a meeting, I told Mikhail I would take care of you for a bit."

"Don't need taken care of, more than capable of doing that myself. I won't say no to some company." I slowly make my way up and she immediately places a pillow behind my back. "Thanks."

"Of course, dear." Her eyes sparkle with mirth as she sits down on the edge of the bed.

" You're their mother."

"I am. I wanted to introduce myself last night, but you were already sleeping. My name is Maria, but you just call me Mama. Mikhail said he'd be locking you down as soon as he can."

"Uhh.. Sure. Where are the kids?" Locking me down huh. Looks like we need to have another talk.

"With my youngest. I believe they are making him work to find them in the garden. All my boys are head over heels for those little ones." She gives a light laugh while dragging a chair closer to sit with me.

"I'm glad all of them are getting along. Going to have to get them back to school soon. They've missed far too many days already." I should feel more guilty for keeping them home but after nearly losing them I don't give a damn. They're my kids and I want to keep them close. Mikhail the smart man that he is wants them just as close.

"Don't fuss about that darling, Mikhail already talked to their school and explained that they would be out for the rest of the year. They set them up with some online classes that start next week."

"Well, that was helpful of him." It takes effort but I keep the irritation off my face. I know that I have to let him make choices about the kids but letting someone else take over without talking to me is making my mamma bear wake up.

She just laughs noticing the frustration that seeps through.. "All the boys tend to take charge. Don't hold it against him he wants all of you taken care of."

"There's plenty of other things I'd argue about before making a stink over that. He'll figure my limits out." Biting my lips keeps the laughter in check as we share matching grins.

"As he should. Can't give all our cards away now can we." Oh, I'm going to like this woman.

We spend the better part of three hours talking before the door bursts open and the kids spill through. Hunter pulls Josey in by her arm. Matching laughter erupts as they scramble to hide under my bed. I will never get over hearing that sound.

A younger version of Mikhail hurries in after them. Hands up like claws as he stalks the kids. "You can't run from your dyadya monster. You must pay the toll for your transgressions."

One timed step at a time he goes around the entire room avoiding the bed at each turn. "Come out come out where you are my little nibblers," he sings as the kids bubble over with humor again. Josey's giggle is muffled quickly. I assume Hunter covers her mouth as a shh hisses in the air.

"Dyadya monster is so hungry. Where did his nibblers go?" He spots the tip of my girl's foot that is just poking out with a big grin. His eyes dart up to me with a wink.

Keeping quiet we watch him stomp noisily calling for the kids to come out for several minutes. He continues calling, getting slightly softer as he moves lightly closer and closer. Sinking to his knees he slides forward til he is within reach of her foot. A quick strike and he's pulling her shirking form out. Fingers attack her ribs and raspberries blow into her neck.

"No dyadya!" She shouts. "Hunter help me!"

In a flash, my boy reappears and jumps on the man's back. Shouts and laughter fill the air while we sit back and enjoy the show. Hunter wraps his arms around his neck, and he drops to the floor with a mock shout of surprise.

The door bangs off the wall as Mikhail charges in with the twins at his back. "What is going on in here?" Exhaustion drips in Mikhail's voice as he crosses his arms and glares at the tangle of bodies.

"Kail! Dyadyas!" Wiggling from under to two over top of her, Josey jumps straight into him, forcing him to quickly catch her before she falls. "Save us from the monster!"

Vlad steps forward and plucks her from Mikhail's arms, allowing the other two to join the tussle happening on the carpet. I take the time to study the oldest. Through the hard mask he wears, I can see deep pain and longing. His expression softens as soon as he holds her in his arms. Maria is right; the kids have all the men wrapped tightly around their little fingers.

She is quick to tuck her head under his chin. Mid whisper to my little girl, he catches me watching. His voice is deeper than his brother's as he says, "I'm sorry for Nikolai barging into the room. He isn't fully housebroken as of yet."

"Hey! I heard that, brat!" Nikolai yells from the headlock Mikhail has him in to allow Hunter to take revenge.

"How are you feeling, sestra?" Vlad doesn't acknowledge the yell as steps to the side of the bed.

"Contrary to what everyone else thinks, I'm fine.; just sore. Shut up Mikhail," I growl when he raises his head to contradict me.

The brothers laugh as he closes his mouth with a silent grumble.

Chapter 37

I have gotten lucky that Ember has not fought me about staying in our bed to allow her ribs to heal without any added stress. Every second of every hour I can keep her willingly in there gives my heart just a bit more room to breathe easier. Her tolerance to my worrying over her hasn't escaped my notice. This isn't going to last much longer.

Mother has not been as hard to keep at bay as all of us thought. The moment she walked into the kitchen where my children sat with their uncle she was in love. Her focus was on keeping them entertained so that Ember could rest without interruption. Not that Ember was thrilled with the kids not coming to her when they needed something,

She let it go without a fight after my mother came in to see her. Neither of them would let me in the room while they talked. Once the kids calmed down they kicked us all out. I will probably come to regret that in the future.

The first few days Ember slept more than she was awake, so it took some time for them to have that longer conversation. Mother finally has a daughter to dote on and she is fiercely enjoying it. None of us has ever seen her so giddy. I'm sure she was worried that not one of us would give her any grand babies so now she wants to hold them as much as possible.

After Nicolas, she was unable to try for the little girl she so desperately wanted, and it shows. Ember is not going to be amused by the vast volume of dresses now lining the closet in our daughter's room. All I can be grateful for is that my little girl isn't a large fan of glitter. Not sure if the amount of pastels is any better.

"Milaya what are you doing?" My little girl is tucked under the bench just outside of Vlad's office coloring away in the book my coldest brother gave her. Damn big softie.

"Waiting for dyadya Vlad to come out and play with me." A grin spans her face as she spots me. Rushing forward she gives me a crushing hug for a five-year-old before returning to her original place to continue the picture.

"That could be hours from now Josey. We are very busy looking for the people who hurt Mommy and Hunter. Why

227

don't you go see where Babushka and your brother are?"

"Dedushka took them out an hour ago."

"Why did you not go with them?" Why would they not tell me they were taking my son out without asking me first?

"Didn't want to go. Wanted to stay here with you and mommy." Her little shoulders shrug without stopping.

"Mommy is sleeping right now. Why don't you come with me?" Kneeling, I hold my hand out for her knowing she jumps at every chance to be with my brothers and I.

She jumps back up and flies into my arms with a round of happy giggles. So easy to make a smile that lights up my world. Standing we make our way through the door without another word. Vlad will be annoyed but he will get over it. He already has a soft spot for the one grinning happily at him as I set her on the couch with her book and crayons.

"Mikhail, pochemu ona ne s mamoy," Vlad growls giving me a pointed look.

Yep, not the happiest, but he won't throw a fit with her in the room. It might be a good thing she is here as a reminder of what we stand to lose if the ones responsible aren't taken care of. "She did not want to leave the house with them."

He scowls at me, though his eyes soften as they flick to Josey. "Milaya, if you can sit here without making a peep, you can stay."

"Yes, dyadya Vlad." She flashes him a beaming smile. It takes effort to hide the smile as I watch him study my daughter. The man will never admit it, but hearing her use his Russian title gets the straight-laced stickler every time. He can't help but turn to goo every time she bats those lashes at him.

"Zatknis', brat," Vlad snaps. Dimitri and I grin at each other as he ruffles Josey's hair before sitting next to me.

We lose track of time going over every fact we have on the group who took my family. Admittedly it isn't near enough to track the bastards down yet. Viking has had no more luck than we have. All of our channels have gone dead on the group.

"Kail, I'm hungry." My little girl pokes her head over the side of my chair.

We all jump having forgotten that she was in the room. As one we turn to the clock, startled to see that we've been sitting here for five hours. Had we really ignored her for so long? Why hadn't she said anything earlier? How did Ember raise such well behaved kids?

"I'm sorry Milaya, you were so quiet we forgot you were here." I stand and pull her up to kiss her cheek. "Let's head to the kitchen to get Mommy something to eat too."

"Come on, dyadyas,." she demands of my brothers with a sweep of her hand.

"Josey, I'm sure they have more work to do first." I try to

distract her as they both raise their brows at us. No one but our parents have ever demanded anything of us since Vlad became the head of our family.

"Momma says you have to eat to have brain power, and they ate before I did this morning," she says giving them the sink eye.

"Our plemyannitsa is right; we need to give our brains some time to recharge." Dimitri stands, quickly stealing her from my arms and tossing her onto his back. All her volume makes itself known as she shrieks for more. Why does he like making her scream so loud.

"Hhaa… we will come back to this tomorrow. Talking in circles is getting us nowhere." Vlad sighs but follows us out, eating up the space with long strides to steal Josey from his twin.

"Dyadya, I want Vlad!" Her legs kick out at Dimitri when he tries to keep her. It only takes a second for her to be traded. She's tucked under his chin causing the rock of the man to crack a tiny smile.

Dimitri pouts as he attempts to get her back. "Give me back, moya plemyannitsa."

"No. Do not be greedy, little brother." He bounces my daughter in his arms as we make our way to the kitchen. The man was made to be a father.

"When will you stop holding that above me? I was five minutes behind you!"

"Da and you still are. You set yourself up from the beginning."

Chapter 38

The house is quiet as I make my way down the stairs. His parents must have taken the kids out again because the only voices I can make out are the men inside Vlad's closed office. Just got to get past that door without them knowing I'm up and around. Good things I'm a master of stalking and getting around unseen.

Three weeks looking at nothing but the walls of that bedroom is quite enough. My ribs don't even ache from getting cleaned up and throwing on a pair of Mikhail's boxes and another of his shirts. I could live in his things. Now if only my damn man would believe me when I say that I'm fine. This is the most freedom I've had, and I don't want to lose it just yet.

Slowing down my pace I pass that door and continue until after several doors I finally find the kitchen. The space is wide open. Stainless Steele appliances blend in with the modern rustic charm. Gray cabinets and garnet counter tops look amazing together. No reason to be jealous of the man's space but damn!.

Ilya and Maskin look up from cleaning their guns as I push my way inside. Parts lay on the table in neat lines ready to be reassembled. The smell of gun oil was thick in the air even with the window open. Classic military men. I'd still like to know where the hell my knife went to. I'm not going to be able to make a duplicate. One dream, one blade. That's how it's always been. Not the time to think about it right now. Where's the real food.

"Don't move." I give both the stink eye as they go to get up. Their asses drop back down without another word. "I'm perfectly fine. I've humored all of you long enough. I can't stay in that bed a moment longer without going crazy."

"Did you need something Mat'?" Ilya smiles as he watches me move further into the open space. Maskin goes back to working on the parts in front of them although I still feel his eyes on me.

"Mat' is not my name boy," I sigh rolling my eyes.

"It means mother," Maskin tells me without looking up.

I stop short and think about it for a minute before accepting the term. Shrugging I continue on with my search for real food. "Sounds correct."

"What are you looking for," Ilya asks again.

"Something besides the damn soup and light meat Mikhail repeatedly brings me." I try not to grumble too harshly as he's listening to what the doctor told him. It's just three weeks of very little solid food that is about to drive me crazy. My body needs meat protein to return to normal. I doubt that I will be able to stay civil for more than another day. Opening a door I'm happy to have found the fridge. Damn there's a ton of food here. Why have I been getting the shitty choices.

"Third shelf down has the roast from lunch. Plates are right behind you," Ilya winks going back to work.

I nearly rip the handle from the door in my hurry to get to the promised feast and there it is. My mouth is watering at the sight of thick slices of beef. A plate and utensils are in my hand faster than lightning. A large slab of beef and three heaping scoops of vegetables fill the available space till none is left.

"Don't want to heat that up?" Ilya laughs at my face as he watches me plop into the chair beside Maskin.

"And give Mikhail more time to find me and take it? Fuck that." Knife and fork make short work of chunking up the meat into bite-size pieces. That first bite drags a loud sexual sounding moan from my lips. Dear God, this tastes amazing! If he doesn't start giving me the good stuff, I might choke him.

"Ember-Lee what the hell are you doing out of bed!" Mikhail's voice booms around the walls of the room. The twins stand behind him, Vlad is again holding Josey.

"Eating." I shovel another bite in my mouth and moan again completely ignoring the furious man stomping my way.

"You are going to make yourself sick."

"Could happen but it tastes great." My shoulders lift as I stuff some potatoes and carrots in. I don't know who cooked this but I'm willing to kiss ass to be fed like this every day. Don't tell my mom. She wouldn't be happy if I said someone else's food was better.

"I will get you something just give me your plate." He stands over me with hands on his hips and a scowl on his face. A muscle in his jaw ticks as I continue to eat.

"You reach for this plate you better be ready to have a hole in your hand," I threaten.

"Ember, give me that plate now." His hand appears at the edge of the ceramic, and I lash out with my knife while I take another bite. All movement around us stops as every eye turns towards the table.

Mikhail stares down at the line of blood slowly dripping to the table from the shallow slash on his hand. His eyes slowly climb to mine; the blue swirling with heat as he stares at me. His nostrils flaring but he doesn't make a sound.

"I told you not to touch my food." The fork reaches for another bite.

"Josey, stay with your dyadyas." His tone is dead flat causing me to look up mid-chew. Well, shit.

Before I can blink, his hand is on my arm pulling me from my seat. All I can do is squeak around the half-chewed beef as he lifts me off the floor. Gripping my ass and thighs making me wrap my legs around his hips, so I don't fall before heading for our room. All I can do is cling to him as the men start laughing from the room we left. I can hear my daughter ask what's going on.

I vaguely see his parents and Hunter walk through the doors as Mikhail kicks ours shut behind us. My back meets the mattress, and his hips lock me in place without putting any pressure on my healing ribs. Reaching behind his head, he strips his shirt off, revealing a glorious expanse of his tattooed chest to my first clear view. Metal clicks as he slowly opens the clasp of his belt and drags everything down so quickly that his hips barely leave mine.

Buttons go flying as he rips the front of my shirt open. I don't get a chance to breathe as he pulls the knife from his belt. The same one I left for him at the hotel. His eyes hold mine as he cuts his own boxers from me. The blade moves in a lazy dance just brushing my lightly bruised ribs for a moment before he sinks the blade two inches deep into the headboard over us. The wood shakes the bed from the force of the impact.

"If you wanted my attention, moya lyubov'." He starts and than pauses as he raises his bloody hand between us to lick at the red line clean. His mouth lowers to plunder mine with rough strokes. The taste of copper coats my tongue as he pulls me out to play. Holy shit I'm glad I'm not wearing any panties right now. "All you had to do was ask."

"Thank God! I was wondering when you'd snap out of the coddling bullshit." Latching on to the scruff at his jaw, I pull him down to weld our lips together. I've needed to feel him above me since I woke up in that damn hospital room.

"One hint of pain and I stop."

Those are not words I want to hear from his lips. "Mikhail, my ribs haven't been a problem for nearly a week. Now shut the hell up and make love to me."

His big hand curls around the back of my head; his eyes soften with a warm smile. "You are the mother to two beautiful healthy children, and you are carrying our third. The moment you returned to my arms; covered in blood is not something that I am going to forget any time soon. I was terrified that I had gotten there too late."

"Mikhail…" I reach up and brush the fallen hair out of his eyes. "I can't change what's already happened, but honestly, I wouldn't change anything that has happened between us. I don't know how to be anyone but who I've always been."

"I never want you to change, moye plamya. Seeing you in that state has upended my whole life, so if I want to coddle you, I will damn sure do so."

Lifting my arms above my head I wiggle down suggestively to lay out comfortably beneath my big bad man. "So, get to coddling your wife, husband."

"Mm, I love it when you call yourself my wife. Hearing you claim me makes my blood burn." Those firm lips land on the pulse on my neck. His chest presses against my naked aching nipples and the hard outline of his cock nestles against my stomach. "We will be making that change official very soon."

"Not until you give me ten orgasms and a ring," I tease nipping at his cheek.

Latching on to the skin he sucks at the junction of my shoulder, slowly moving his way up to suck my ear with soft scrapes of his teeth. "Is that a challenge, moye plamya?"

"Does it sound like a challenge, Mikhail Sokolov?" My brow goes up. Please take the bait. Lord please make him break right now.

"Then I had better get started, hadn't I? Good thing you know I can deliver on my promises, isn't it, detka?" Daft finger skim down my sides to grip my hips and I'm airborne. My body comes to a stop to leave me staring at the headboard only inches from my nose.

"Sit," he demands pulling me down.

As if I'm going to make it easier on him. Lowering just shy of his waiting mouth I lean back arching my back. Gripping the wood in front of me I wiggle dropping down for just a moment to give him a brief taste of what he wants. "Make me."

His hands leave my thighs to deliver two stinging open-palmed slaps to each of my ass cheeks. Unwilling to let me play anymore his grip squeezes the flesh of my ass and pulls me down to his hungry tongue. I can't help the moan that leaves my lips as my hips jerk in time to his assault on me. That damn tongue of his knows exactly where to press into my sensitive clit. Four months without his expert touch is going to do me in far too soon.

"Slower." My breath is nothing but pants already and he has barely touched me. I need it to last longer. I need it now! I need something to hold me up. Gripping the headboard I lean back to give him more room.

"Next time." His voice is more of a vibration than sound as he works me higher. Teeth graze over my clit and then he sucks it between his lips with hard pulls.

"Shit!" Too much. I can't hold back the edge as it rushes through me. My knees pin his head tightly in the valley of my legs, and my body curls into a ball as I scream above him. I can't seem to control my body as it falls forward shivering violently, pulsing in waves.

Sliding me back into the cradle of his lap he sits up to lean against the wood. His arms hug me close to feather his fingers up and down my spine. "Nine more."

Chapter 39

Ember lays limp in my arms mindlessly tracing the tattoos down my ribs. Her lashes flutter against my pecs drowsily, hanging on the edge of wakefulness. The sensation lulling lulls me to the edge of sleep as well. Time needs to stand still. I don't think I've ever been more at peace. Our children are safe and happy. My woman is in my arms. Even with the threat of the traffickers my life is as close to perfect as it can be right now.

"When did you get this?"

A small smile pulls at my lips knowing which one she's asking about from just her touch. The only link to her memory besides the knife I now carry everywhere. A mother gray wolf curls around her litter of pups while the male with blue eyes stands guard over them. The adults' heads are pressed together as they watch the babies below them.

"Three weeks ago."

The bed shifts as she rolls on top of me. "Why?"

Opening my eyes, I watch her through the curtain of hair surrounding us. "Because I knew I had found what I wanted. I wanted to have a piece of our family with me at all times."

Green darkens the blue as she frowns down at me. "You forget how wolves operate."

Tilting my head, I wait for her to continue.

Leaning forward she kisses the tip of my nose with a little laugh. "They need their family to prosper." Her finger dips over the image where the male and female's heads touch. "They need to be present for all the things that are to come. Most important the female will protect the male just as strongly as he protects her."

Leaning up, I bring my lips to hers in a slow exploration filled with intent and promise. Sitting us both up so that I can reach into my end table without her seeing what I have.. The small blue box slides eagerly into my fingers as I bring it between us. "I know now that we are stronger together. I will not leave you like that again. Marry me, moya lyubov'."

Her eyes widen as they land on the box. The lid opens to reveal the simple slim golden band inlaid with several small round diamonds. "Mikhail!" Her hands cup over her mouth muffling her surprise.

"I had it made so that it would not create a danger to you as you worked in your forge." I pull it out and tilt it, so the light catches the words inscribed on the inside of the band.

Her brows shot up. "You're going to let me work?"

"Eventually," I laugh with a shrug.

"What does it say?"

"Ty plamya moygeo serdtsa. You are the flame of my heart. Marry me, Ember. Keep my heart burning for you and our children," I whisper with baited breath.

Tears glitter in her eyes as I wait, sitting on the bed naked as the day I entered the world. Her swirling eyes burn into mine as she weighs everything that she sees and what I said. A sob bubbles up and out of her lips before she lunges forward. Arms catch my head in a hug before loosening so she can pull back to pepper my face with kisses.

"Is that a, yes?" I grip the hair at the back of her head to hold her still enough to answer the question that needs to be spoken this second.

"Yes! Yes, I will marry you, Mikhail," she yells through her laughter.

Joyous relief washes over me as I pull her close again. Lush lips easily part under the demand of my own. Not releasing any part of her, I take us back to the mattress. Her hands grip my back, nails biting lightly into the back of my neck.

Chapter 40

It's been six weeks since Hunter and I had been taken but it feels like a lifetime ago. So much of my world has been changed since the arrival of a certain demanding Russian man pacing through the windows of the house as he searches for me. Jokes on him, I'm not inside. Few more minutes of peace and quiet before he figures out where I am and the sun feels good on my back.

I was positive that there would only be one great love in my life and that with him gone I was destined to spend the rest of my time here without another to share my life with. I had my kids and was taking time for myself again. I was content and enjoying life. Hell, I am so far ahead with orders that taking these time off to relax isn't going to matter.

God is surely laughing at my thoughts, and I can't say that I mind it too awful much. These last weeks haven't been the smooth sailing many around us thought they were. I had to put my foot down more than once at the overbearing protectiveness of my soon-to-be husband.

After the night he gave the ring to me I had hoped he would settle down and allow me to explore the house without him breathing down my neck about me being on my feet for so long. More than once he would find me doing things, that he thought I shouldn't be doing just yet and my ass would be dragged back to the room where he persuaded me to pass out for a time. The man is very gifted in that area. I may be misbehaving just to get one of his lectures.

Maskin's phone goes off and I know that my time alone is about to be over. The big man never strays far from my side. I don't mind it as much as I thought that I would. I appreciate that he's just a silent shadow no matter what I end up doing. I know he lets Mikhail know where I am if he asks but he never tells me I can't do something. I even started setting up a forge in one of the back outbuildings and he hasn't told anyone yet.

"The point of giving you a phone was so that when I need you, I don't have to hunt for you." His presence next to me doesn't last long as large arms fall on either side of my arms to cage me between him and the ground.

"Property isn't that big, but we can go out to the woods if you'd really like to go for a hunt." I keep my eyes closed enjoying the rare sunny day.

"Where is your phone, moye plamya," his lips tickle over my

ear as he leans in to whisper his question.

"Room."

"Is it so difficult to keep it on you?"

"We had a single cell for when we go to events. They aren't reliable in the terrain I go through. Not something that I ever had to worry about keeping on me before."

Groaning, he drops his head into my hair. "Yes, but we aren't there. Now we will have to be quick before your parents arrive."

I'm in the air before I can utter a single word. All I can do is laugh and hold on. The world spins as he throws me over his shoulder as he runs us past the cluster of rose bushes, oriental pines, and into the large willows that screen us from the house. My feet hit the ground at the same time the palms of my hands manage to brace us against the rough tree bark. Hot persistent lips suck on my neck while his hands work to push my pants over my hips. His fingers grip my flesh hard enough to make me groan. I love that he isn't treating me like I'm going to break anymore.

Gripping my throat, he pulls me back and sinks into me with one hard thrust. "Fuck!" The word is barely a whisper with the little air that he allows to flow around his fingers. He catches me as I stumble forward, cradling the bottom swell of our baby.

"Quiet." His breath fans over my ear as he picks up his pace. When one of his brothers' yells for us I giggle as he goes faster.

It's hard to be keep my approval to myself when he keeps hitting every sensitive ridge inside me. Each long pull nearly takes him from me before battering back inside. His teeth graze over my ear before latching on to the sensitive skin sending me right over the edge. I can't keep everything in as I moan, "Mikhail!"

He grunts through the next few strokes before emptying

himself into my shaking form. His hips keep up slow thrusts as he pants into my neck. "You are a drug, moye plamya. I cannot get enough of you."

"Fuck!" My insides clench as he slips out of me.

Tucking me back into my clothes before himself, we are presentable by the time Nikolai finds us walking out holding hands. My hair may be a bit mussed up but I can't do anything about it now but play it cool.

His eyes dance over me before speaking. "Sestra, tvoi roditeli i bray zdes'."

"I swear all of you men are bound to make me guess at every little thing that comes out of your mouths." I glare at my soon-to-be-younger brother. "I was already told they were here, but thank you, little Nikki."

His smile falls. "That is not my name sister."

"It is now," I chuckle.

"Mikhail, are you going to let her speak to me like that?"

Face devoid of emotion he gives me a kiss. "Go see you parents."

"Planned to, have fun boys," I smirk and give him another kiss. I leave the men to bicker over my choice of nicknames while I head to go hunting for my parents.

Chapter 41

The kids disappear up the stairs to bed with Mikhail trailing them to get ready for bed as I watch them from the couch. Since we arrived here, he has made it a habit to put the kids to bed every night. It's his way of spending some time with them after meeting with his brothers all day. There still haven't been any new leads but they are busy with their other businesses as well.

Josey loves this. She has been latched onto the big man since day one. She does regularly abandon him for one of the twins, however. I'm sure Vlad is her go to if Mikhail isn't around much to Dimitri's displeasure. She's loving all the male attention. Hunter is more cautious but since their talk in the hospital, he isn't hostile towards him when he's told to do things. When he isn't checking in on me, he's following his new grandparents.

The guys and their father do make a point of taking each of them out by themselves for a number of things to keep the kids busy. I'm still not over the amount of purple that now takes up space in Josey's room. It took a few nights but we finally got the two of them to sleep in their own rooms.

"He seems like a good man." I jump, having been caught up in my head to spot my mom at the end of the couch.

"He is. It's hard to miss how much he loves the kids." I can't help the laugh that comes out. "Josey has them all wrapped around her finger. Hunter isn't pushing back as hard as I thought he would."

"That boy is just like you. Mikhail and his family have something in them that all of you respond to. I've waited a long time to see you so happy again. It puts my heart at ease knowing you have someone like him."

"You don't think I'm moving too fast?"

"Do you believe that you are?" She turns to face me. Her head resting on her elbow across the back of the cushion as her gray eyes shine as she looks at me.

"Sometimes the doubt tries to creep in," I whisper playing with the ring on my finger. The simple diamonds and emeralds flash in the firelight. "Everyone in town already says I'm crazy, so I don't really care what others think mostly."

"Ember honey," Strong fingers lift my gaze back to hers. "The only true question you need to ask is does he make you happy?"

Smiling, I swallow around the tears that want to form. "Since the first moment." And I realize he does above all else. "He makes me feel alive and loved. Protected, like nothing can get to me ever again."

"Well, then there you have your answer. Let the town folks talk. Only you can live your life." Her smile turns into a grin, and she crooks a finger at me to get me closer. "I knew your father was the one the third time I socked him."

"No!" I bite back the bark of laughter with my hands. "You punched dad?"

"Sure did! Was after me for a month before he left for boot camp. Every time I punched him, he'd grin and ask for my number like we were just saying hello. I barely went a week without any letters when he left for the war." Every ounce of the little woman before me glows with pride.

"I can't believe you let him get away with that."

"Oh, I let him know how I felt when he got home. Don't you worry about that, honey." She pats my hand before standing up. "Now come on you need your sleep before the chaos starts tomorrow."

"I never thought I'd get married again," I grumble unfolding myself from the comfy seat with some difficulty. My little girl rolls upset at me for moving. Laughing I rub over her small form. "Didn't expect this surprise to happen again either."

"I couldn't be happier for the blessing." Maria nearly dances into the room with her never-ending smile. "After what happened with the woman meant for Vlad, I did not think any of my boys would ever settle down."

I want to ask more about what happened, but I don't dare as she and Mom each grab one of my arms. "Is this really necessary?"

Mom pats my arm and Maria laughs as they march me out of the sitting area and towards the room set aside for me tonight. "Tradition my dear. He must pay his due to be worthy of you and the children."

"Sure he already did that with finding me and Hunter," I try to protest but even to me it's weak.

Maria cackles so hard I'm amazed she doesn't break an ankle. "Oh no, he has much more to prove to be good enough for you."

"Joe and Dad are going to have way too much fun with this ransom," I groan to hide my own amusement. If I know my brother, he'll come up with several massively embarrassing tasks for Mikhail to perform before he's allowed to see me walk down the aisle. With the added instigators in his own family and he may not be ready for what's coming his way.

"My son is a big boy. He will handle the pranks just fine."

Chapter 42

Of all the things to tell Viking about our wedding traditions Dimitri had to gush about the ransom. If I wasn't going to be legally binding my woman to me in a matter of hours, I might just kill all of them. I guess I can start calling him by name now that we are about to be family. It may just tick him off enough to make the day entertaining for me.

Spending the night away from Ember has not been comfortable. I barely managed to doze off at best. For once I'm grateful that Josey had a nightmare and came to spend the night with me, or I would not have gotten any sleep at all. The day has been too long as is with all the pranks my brothers new and old have put me through. Those assholes even got Hunter in on their games first thing this morning. My own son. I shake my head as I step out of the shower.

Such a simple innocent note should not have ended with me covered in that ungodly amount of chocolate sauce and pink feathers. I should have seen through the invitation to meet all the men for a drink in the den. Today of all days, I should have seen something like this coming. But no I never thought that my own boy would do something so dirty to me.

I swear I will find every last picture those gryaznyye ublyudki took of me floundering in the mess they caused and burn all of them from existence. They will pay dearly for the ridiculous amount of time it took me to scrub myself clean. They will also buy me another bottle of shampoo. I'm just glad we have such a large water heater. Cold water would have made it harder to get clean.

Only my girls will be spared my retaliation after this day is over. Hunter, my brave little son, will not. I won't do to him what I plan for his uncles, but the knowing smirk he tried to hide will see that he is suitably taken to task for his part. I can't be truly mad that he is finding his space within the family. Pride lightens my heart to see him holding his own.

Slipping on my suit jacket I stop short as a knock sounds from the door. "Da."

"Brat." Vlad steps in and looks at me with a small smile. The happiest expression I'd seen on his face in years that didn't happen without Josey in his arms.

"Syn," Father steps in behind him, his left side still slightly dragging after all these years. His eyes shine as he steps up to

250

me and straightens my tie. "It is time."

"I am ready." I can't help the smile that pulls my lips up as I think about Ember meeting me at the end of the aisle. "After you." Adjusting my cuffs I follow them out the door and down the stairs to the garden where my woman wanted to hold the ceremony.

The scent of lilacs slams into my lungs the instant I step out into the bright green of the spring grass. It's likely that when I walk out of here a married man, I will have one hell of a headache. One word from Ember of what her favorite flower is and mother has managed to cover the space in every color of bloom she could get her hands on.

There are petals on the cloth laid down for Ember to walk on. Tule sheets with ribbons hang off the chairs filled with friends and family. A vine-covered arch stands at the front waiting for us to say our vows under. Mother has managed to pull off a full wedding in just three short weeks and cover it in lilacs.

"Did someone throw up a flower shop back here?" Nikolai wrinkles his nose while taking in the area.

"Brat." Vlad's voice is a low rumble of warning from beside me as my hand connects with the back of our baby brother's head.

"Don't you just love how everything turned out," Mother rushes up to us gushing. "I know it is not perfect. If I had had some more time, I could have had everything perfect. I'm not sure I have enough flowers."

"It is perfect," I hug her to my side and drop a quick kiss to her hair. "Ember will love it."

Tears well in her eyes. Her hands grip my jaw pulling me down to kiss my head. "This is your day too, moy syn." A few heavy pats land on my checks before she spins away and is gone in a flash of purple velvet.

A waving hand catches my attention as the preacher motions me to the front. We all take our places and turn to the house to wait for my woman to make her way outside. She can't come out quick enough for me. If I had it my way, this big ceremony wouldn't be happening. All I need is for her tied to me for the rest of our lives.

I watch with pride as Hunter, holding the rings, escorts his sister as she throws fistfuls of more lilac petals onto the ground. My girl practically bounces towards me with a huge grin. The bright red velvet of her dress snaps angrily around her ankles with each wild step. My little ones' light shines so brightly it makes my heart ache.

Josey throws herself into my legs when they reach me. I barely get my arms around her before she darts off to take her place. My boy gives me a shy smile as he moves to my side. Ever the little soldier. I drop a hand to his shoulder for a squeeze just as we hear the music start up.

My head snaps to attention, and I feel my heart stop. Ember steps out and I can't breathe. The white gown hugs her body with each gentle sway of her hips. Swatches of red highlight each curve to perfection. She is absolutely beautiful. My beautiful, gorgeous, perfect woman. Thank you for this woman Lord.

Before I feel like I get one breath in she's suddenly by my side. Her hand slips from her father's into my own. He says something but I don't even try to take in the words. All that matters is the one standing in front of me.

"Moye plamya." My words are barely audible and only for her ears. The back of my fingers skim over the soft warm flesh of her cheek as I lift the gauzy veil, so it falls over the waterfall of curl behind her. "Are you ready, moya lyubobv'?"

Our heads meet as she pulls me down for a quick kiss. The green and blue whirl in equal measures of warmth as she smiles up at me. "Damn right."

"Get on with it, Father." I don't take my eyes off her as I wave for the priest to get moving with the formalities.

The man chuckles and easily opens the pages of the bible in his hands. "It will go faster if I have your attention, my son."

Damn, man doesn't even flinch as I whip around to scowl at him. He simply smiles completely undisturbed by the murder written on my face. "Son, I have been with your family for years, that look doesn't scare me."

"Mikhail." Ember's small fingers squeeze in mine to pull my attention back to her. "Leave the man along long enough to marry us, will ya?"

"For you."

"No blood in front of the kids."

Flicking my eyes to both our children, I calm my irritation. The demons grumble but calm down at her say so. She's right. That side of my world isn't something they ever need to see if it can be helped. My princess is too innocent and beautiful to see me hurt someone. It's unfortunate that my brilliant son has already seen death.

Chapter 43

I can't help the smug grin I sport as my groom mutters under his breath about disrespectful churchmen. When it comes to anything other than my health, he is a total teddy bear. One word and he turns into pudy in my hands.

"Carry on Father," I whisper at Mikhail's scowling frown.

"Thank you, my dear." The old man's face breaks open in a cheery grin. Smile lines are etched deep into his heavy face. "Now then where was I?"

Mikhail swings his head to look at the man again ready to say something else nasty. Tossing the bunch of lilacs to one of the bodies behind me, I grip his face between my hands and pull him back to me. "Play nice."

Sighing he lays his forehead to mine. "For you. For now."

Without breaking contact, we wave for the man to continue. A smile stretches his lips as we stare at each other. Fingers ghost down my arms before linking tightly within my own. Neither of us can look away from the other as vows are spoken and rings exchanged.

Mikhail doesn't wait for the Father to tell him he's allowed to kiss me. I'm swung around and laying over his arm with his lips hungrily feeding on mine. I'm left with no choice but to hold on and meet him stroke for stroke. He pulls me close, fitting our bodies together like glue. There is not a speck of space between us and I'm in heaven.

We reluctantly pull our mouths apart to a whooping crowd cheering at our backs. Tears burn the back of my eyes as the reality that I have bound myself to another man after losing hope of sharing this life with another fills my heart. Jack never would have wanted me to be alone. I'm sure he's cheering the loudest for me.

"We're married." I can't help how breathless my voice sounds.

"We are."

"Damn," My body shakes with excitement. I can't help but kiss him again. "I love you."

"And I love you." His big hand cups the sides of my face. "Our story is just beginning."

The family help make quick work of swapping the rows of chairs out for tables and a seemingly endless amount of food. I swear, the boards should be groaning under the massive weight forced upon them. I don't want to even try to count the number of different dishes. It would take me most of the day to get through it all.

My two terrors are racing around the trees with the other children. Every now and then I caught a glimpse of Nikolai and Dimitri in the mix. With how much food they consumed, I would have bet that they would be in a food coma by now. I know I nearly am, and I didn't eat half of what they did. It doesn't hurt that I have a devilishly handsome husband who is currently holding my bare feet in his lap. Big fingers dig deep to release the tense tissue of the swelling flesh.

"I want to make it official." He doesn't look up as he keeps working.

"You just married me; I think we are as official as marriage gets."

"Our children."

"What about them?" I groan as he hits a tender spot in my arch.

"I want them to legally be mine. I do not want someone to tell me I cannot be where they are or that I can't make choices for their safety if you aren't there."

My mouth opens and closes, but I can't make a sound come out. Just when I think this man can't get any better, he has to take my feet from under me. Snapping my mouth shut I work on holding back my tears.

He stops rubbing at the first leaking tear. Leaning in he wipes it away and goes back to work. "I told you from the start that I wanted every piece of you. I love you and our children. Will you let me do this?"

Sniffing back the lump trying to take over my throat I reach down and pull his gaze to meet mine again. "It takes more than blood to be family, and I know you will go to hell and back for us."

"Every time."

"Then you already know the answer from me. Now you need to go ask our kids." His face lights up like the sun as he nods.

The chair next to me whines on the stone as Dimitri tosses himself down gasping for air. "Bog! Do your little ones run on unending batteries sastra?"

"With the day they've had and the insane amount of food, it won't be long before they crash," I say with a grin and give my husband a wink.

"And it will not be long now." Mikhail rests his arm over the back of my chair to squeeze my shoulder. "They are bringing the cake out momentarily."

"And the added sugar will have them dropping like flies in

under an hour." I tip my glass of tea to clink against my his as we share a secret smile.

The big man sits up straighter as he spots the answer to his wavering energy being placed on the table. "I'll round up my little ones!" He's out of the chair and running before either of us can get a word out.

The entire herd of children scream from their cover and come running. Josey and Hunter race for us as Mikhail helps me up. They collide with our legs, nearly knocking us over. Reaching down, we each pick up one of them and squish them between us in a hug.

"Cake Mommy!" The girl nearly vibrates herself out of my arms in her excitement. "I want some cake."

"I didn't notice." Keeping a straight face is difficult in the face of her energy.

"Let us go cut our cake so that these two are sweetened up extra well for their grandparents." My husband tosses a wink on my way while the troublemakers cheer loudly in our ears.

Once they are on the ground, he wraps me up against him and softens his voice so only I can hear. "Then we can make the most of our alone time together."

"Sounds perfect." A quick kiss to his cheek becomes longer as he takes over. Pushing him back, I smack his chest lightly in mock anger. "Let's get this done. I'm ready to get someplace without all these people."

"Soon, moye plamya, I promise." Taking my hand, he leads me to our bouncing kids and pulls me so that I'm cradled between his arms.

Never letting go he moves to pick up the knife. A small twist and the blade is in my hand with his guiding over top mine. Our people surround us calling out well wishes. I tune them out and focus on the task at hand. The tip of the blade glides with the ease of going through hot butter as we make the first cut. Lifting it for the second cut, it sinks in with the same ease.

Cake splatters across us as the thing explodes. I'm on the ground with Mikhail covering me before I get the air for any type of reaction. I hear the kids scream and race to the twins behind us. Men shout and cover the women around them as they pull guns looking for the threat.

Someone shouts that the area is clear. People slowly gather themselves and pull the women back to their feet.

My husband jumps up and helps me up. "Are you alright?" Frantic hands run over everything of me that he can reach.

I grab his hands and give them a firm shake to snap him back to me. I wait for his eye. "I'm fine."

"Are you sure? I did not mean to throw you so hard. Is the baby okay?" His eyes flick over me again in panic.

"Promise." One finger draws him back.

He pulls me close before releasing a heavy breath. His hand begins petting my hair to calm himself down. "What the hell happened?"

The twins slide in close, a child holding to each man with large uncertain eyes. Tears run down Josey's face, only slowing as Vlad talks to her.

Dimitri checks all of us visually before promising, "We will find out, brat."

Uncontrollable laughter unexpectedly fills the air. Every single person turns to the source of the sound. Nikolai is bent double holding his stomach with tears pouring from his closed eyes. "That was awesome! I flew farther than I could have dreamed." He wheezes, not taking notice of any of us.

"You fucker." ," I hiss. I can't believe he would be so immature to pull such a stunt with the amount of armed and paranoid people in attendance.

The angry murmur of the crowd seems to reach him. Still wiping his tears, he looks up and sobers up at the looks aimed his way. His eyes dart all around, and a few weak chuckles make their way out. I can visibly see his Adam's apple struggle as he takes us all in.

His eyes meet mine and he jumps back with a shriek. "It was a joke, sastra!" Both hands wave imploringly back and forth as if to hold my anger back.

I don't utter a single word as I growl. My hands clench at my sides as his brother begins cussing him out in Russian. Each weak excuse he tries to get out makes me more and more furious.

"You didn't stop to think! My kids have been through enough this year." My shout makes everyone go silent.

"I'm sorry, sastra!" He forces his tears of shame away as he looks at the kids hanging on to the adults.

"Oh, you will be." A grin spreads as I start towards him. Screaming he spins around and takes off; hoping to outrun me. Whipping the front of the dress over my arm I jump into a run and go after his sorry ass. My bare feet eat up the distance between us.

I hear people shouting behind me to stop. He looks back and screams. His legs work harder hoping to outlast me, but he won't have any luck. His ass is mine and I am damn sure going to collect my due.

"Sastra stop. I am sorry! Leave me alone!"

"Get your ass back here, Nikki!"

"Mikhail, brat, stop your wife!"

"Not a chance," my husband yells from where I left him.

About the Author

M. A. Worrell is a born and bred Pennsylvanian with her heart set for the western skies. Growing up in a rural area she got her love for nature and animals from her time helping on the family dairy farm and pulling logs from the woods to heat her home. As she grew her interests expanded to what every little girl wants. Horses are now a part of her everyday life as she watches her four legged children graze in their pasture. In her spare time when she isn't wrangling her boys or animals, she writes.